T0128522

THE BAD BOY GETS PUNISHED

A sissy maid missy bad boy series, part four

m missy

authorHOUSE®

AuthorHouse™
1663 Liberty Drive
Bloomington, IN 47403
www.authorhouse.com
Phone: 1-800-839-8640

Published by AuthorHouse 5/4/2012

ISBN: 978-1-4685-8782-1 (sc)
ISBN: 978-1-4685-8781-4 (e)

CONTENTS

The third book included; Sabrina getting a strapping and giving a blow job, at the same time.

Ally getting a spanking in front of a witness. Really, really, humiliating for Ally.

We have the first report card of the year opening. Still not good news for Ally, more punishment coming.

Thanksgiving, brings the first really big Cally surprise of part three.

Someone stole my money, who??? surprised everyone.

Cally and I enjoyed the best Christmas eve of our lives.

Christmas day, brings "THE MOST SPECIAL CHRISTMAS" that had everyone, including me, in tears.

I passed fucking my 100th girl just before New Years.

Cally gave up her virginity, But, did she?

The second report card day brings yet another surprise.

Sabrina argued with Cally and now Cally is her Boss, not me anymore.

We learned about what happened in advance of Christmas to make Christmas, "THE MOST SPECIAL CHRISTMAS"

Cally, tells me I am a Bad Boy and wants me to be "her" good boy.

Then there is a real surprise as to who gets a whipping and who does the whipping.

The Last report card of the year.

Cally and left for our cruise together.

A sissy maid missy series, part four

As my life develops in this book, part four, we begin with that surprise cruse that Cally bought for us.

The best and worst weekend of my life, My life falls apart as I get arrested, The Plea Bargain, My sentencing hearing, My new life in the place where I am sent to be punished, the Reform Farm.

My continuing relationship with Cally, much to my surprise, but then Cally is always surprising me and those around us.

Some unusual punishments in an unusual place.

The transformation of me, a young rich BOSS OF THE HOUSE, to a small submissive boy to others.

If you have not read; THE BAD BOY AND HIS FRENCH MAIDS, or THE BAD BOY AND HIS FRENCH MAIDS, TWO, or THE BAD BOY AND HIS FRENCH MAIDS, THREE.

You may wish to read them before reading this book as the development of the characters lives follows a path that would not be understood or enjoyed as much if you start in the middle.

Nevertheless, I had summarized the characters information in the book so it can still be enjoyed as a standalone version.

Hello, my name is Morton and this is my story.

I grew up in southwestern Florida just outside of Naples. My twin sister, Mindy, and I were the only children of wealthy parents. We lived in a big house on approximately 10 acres of woods. The house was about 8000 square feet and had a nice pool with waterfalls, a hot tub, and even a diving board.

At 18 years of age I had the most perfect life I could ever imagine. I was the best tennis player in my high school and maybe in the county. My parents sent me to tennis camp every summer and I had lessons throughout the year as well.

I was a great baseball player, especially an outfielder that Willy Mays would be proud. I lead the team with on base percentage and led the league in walks every year.

My twin sister, Mindy, had the same opportunities that I had and was also an excellent tennis player, she did not play baseball.

We seemed to have all the money in the world as my father apparently made a great living and was very rich. So we never had any concerns that many of the other kids our age had.

Both Mindy and me got new cars for our 18th birthday and I should tell you that I became a point of jealousy from the other kids as I drove a $90,000.00 Jaguar. My sister chose a mustang and the other kids seemed to be ok with that choice.

We both got excellent grades in school without much effort and were both considered to be some of the smartest kids in the school. I was sort of the king of the school as I was very popular and most everyone would follow me with any of my opinions.

Discipline was never a real problem as neither my sister or I ever got into any trouble. We did not even have to help clean the house as our parents had a live in maid.

However, my father graduated near the top of his class at West Point and became an army officer, before he became a business man. So, he had little patience for bad behavior.

He taught my sister and me at an early age that you follow the rules or you get punished, Period. My dad use to tell me that was the way of the world and I may as well learn it when I was young enough to adjust to expectations.

My dad made the rules very clear in advance so there was never any surprises. My Father taught us his ten commandments of life, as my father called them.

One, always be obedient to those you need to obey.

Two, Always be polite, to everyone, all the time, no matter what.

Three, Always be friendly and nice to everyone, all the time.

Four, Always do the right thing, even when it's hard.

Five, Always be generous.

Six, There is no good reason to drink.

Seven, There is no good reason to smoke.

Eight, There is no good reason to take drugs.

Nine, There is not good reason to gamble.

Ten, always be honest with yourself and others.

Mindy and I learned and followed my Father's 10 commandments of life, most of the time, and were both very happy kids. Every time we were punished, it was because we forgot one of those rules.

From the time we were around 6 years old, if we were naughty, my dad would spank us with his hand on our bare bottoms over his knees and make us stand in the corner. After we turned 10, we would get our spankings, which were very rare, with a hardwood hairbrush. That was never something to look forward to.

Overall, over my 10 years of corporal punishment, from being six years old to 10 years old, I was probably spanked 6 times with my dad's hand. That's only 6 times in 4 years, so I was pretty good. My sister was probably spanked only 3 or 4 times.

From age 10 to 13 for me, I was spanked with the hairbrush only twice, that was twice too many for me. My sister, maybe three times.

From age 13 to 17 I did not enjoy my father's spanking brush about 5 times. I did seem to have a little problem as I went thru puberty and got three spankings that one year. Only one before and one after that 14th year. My sister I think only got one more hairbrush spanking when she was 14 and that was it for her.

A spanking from our father was a sure and very unhappy event. Our father believed in two things when it came to a spanking. One, it should hurt more than enough for you ever to think that disobedience is worth the risk again. Two, it should be as embarrassing as possible, as that was sometimes worse than the spanking itself.

Therefore, a spanking in our house was always a public affair. In other words Mindy or me would be spanked in the living room and whichever child was not being spanked was there to watch the one who was getting the spanking.

Additionally, my mother was there, but the worst part was that the maid, Sabrina, was there also. As Sabrina hated me, she never missed a good smile as she watched me get a spanking. I also noticed that when it was my sister turn to get spanked that Sabrina was not around.

As I said, our father made the spankings as embarrassing as possible. First he made us stand in the corner for about 30 minutes before each spanking, sort of advertizing to everyone else that a spanking was on its way.

Then right there in front of everyone, our father would call us to his side, as he sat on the spanking chair, and lower my pants and underwear. In my sister case, it most likely was lowering her panties and flipping her skirt up over her back, but you get the idea.

The end result was that you had your naked butt out there for everyone to see. In my case everyone got to see my penis also which was almost the most embarrassing part.

That part got worse in my later years as I would also get an erection. So for the last 4 or 5 spankings of my life from my father I had to stand there in front of everyone, especially Sabrina, with an erection.

Now, I had no idea at this point in my life what the erection was all about as I could not see where they were any good for anything, but for some reason, I felt embarrassed that I had one.

For some reason also, for the last two spankings that my sister Mindy got, I also got an erection watching her get her ass bared and especially as it was spanked over my dad's lap and Mindy wiggled it all over the place and my dad spanked her so hard and for so long.

I loved looking at her bare butt and even got a look at her pussy lips. Not that I knew what I was really looking at, she was just different from me. But, for some reason I liked to look.

I loved watching Mindy's ass turn all red, then dark red, then sort of purple, and then some black and blue.

Before my father stopped spanking Mindy my penis was throbbing for some unknown reason to me.

I think the part I liked the best was the crying. I really like to hear Mindy cry as the spanking went on and on and on. I liked it the best when Mindy cried so hard that I knew she had lost complete control of herself as the spanking was hurting her so much.

When I was the one getting the spanking, as I said, I was really embarrassed to have my ass bared in front of Mindy and Sabrina, not so much for my mother. In my later spankings, as I stood in the corner waiting for my spanking, I was worried about having an erection in front of Sabrina. I seemed to get an erection just from thinking about how embarrassed I would get later.

But, the worst part was when I started to cry, just like Mindy cried. I was so embarrassed to cry in front of Mindy, but especially in front of Sabrina. Nevertheless, no matter how hard I wanted not to cry, I could not stop myself as my dad spanked me so hard and for such a long time that I could do nothing but lay there over his lap and take my spanking and cry my eyes out.

Our dad believed that a spanking should be long enough and hard enough so that we remembered it for a long time. But, more importantly, he believed that the spanking should hurt so much and that you should be embarrassed so much that you would not take any more chances on ever getting another one.

Our father always met his goal as neither Mindy nor me ever would take a chance at doing anything that would result in getting a spanking. So, we only got a few, a few too many. But, they were rare and only for doing stupid things that for one reason of another we did not seem to stay out of as after all, we were young stupid kids in a way and made stupid mistakes.

After the spanking was over, we were sent back to the corner for another 30 minutes but we had to stand in the corner without any pants or underwear so everyone one could see our well spanked asses. Both Mindy and I still cried for a while from both the pain of the spanking and the embarrassment of having to stand in the corner showing off our spanked asses.

When it was Mindy's turn to stand in the corner, she had to hold up the back of her skirt to show off her spanked ass. I loved sitting in the living room after Mindy got spanked and just looked at her nice plump ass.

As I got older I did realize that my embarrassment did not actually come all that much from the process of the spanking, the baring of my ass, the erection for all to see, or the crying, but rather, I thought the most embarrassing part was that I was there to be spanked for being bad.

I always felt like a bad kid during those times and the embarrassment I felt from feeling like a bad kid was the part that bothered me the most.

Having told you all this, I do not want you to think that Mindy or me felt like our dad was cruel or mean in anyway. He spent most of his time playing with us, teaching us, and loving us.

Looking back on the growing years, we did not ever

smoke, drink, sniff glue, take drugs, or do any of the other stupid things that many of our friends were doing. So, my dad's theory about spanking seemed to ring true and he kept us out of trouble by making us fear spankings.

However, this story, my story to you, started when Mindy and I were 18 years old and our parents were killed when their own private plane crashed in Alaska when they were on vacation and got stuck in a sudden snow storm.

They left all of their assets to my sister and I in a trust fund which amounted to over 10 million dollars. My sister and I would get equal shares of the income from the trust until we were 25 years old and then we would be given our shares of the trust outright. The income amounted to about over 30,000.00 per month for each of us, after taxes.

Now, considering we lived in a fully paid 2 million dollar house we certainly did not need all that money to pay the household bills, so the trustee paid all our bills, gave us each an allowance, and allowed the trust amount to keep on growing.

However, as Mindy and I were just 18 years old, the trust required that we have an adult guardian live with us until we were 21 years old.

My Mother's request within the trust asked us to take in her best friend, Molly, as our guardian, together with her twin daughters, Ally and Cally.

My sister and I agreed to honor our dead Mother's

wishes and have Molly and her twin daughters come live in our house with Molly as our guardian. Molly really needed this break as she did not make very much money and her husband, who left her five years earlier, was not paying any child support.

As both my sister and I knew Molly and her two girls very well, it seemed to be a good fit for everyone as both my sister and I liked the three of them. Our only obligation under the trust fund was to have at least one guardian live with us as Mindy and I were under 21 at the time. So, this solution seemed to be an easy answer.

CAST OF CHARACTORS:

MORTON:

My name is Morton, Mort for short and as I said I was 18 years old. Although I was a very good tennis player and baseball player, I was only five foot seven inches tall but was hoping to get taller in my later teenage years.

However, that may only be a hope and a prayer as my mom was only five foot tall and my dad was only five foot eight inches tall. No one in my mother's or father's family was much taller, so most likely I would end up being just be too short for my own liking.

In addition to being short, I was also small. I only weighed about 125 pounds and had a 28 inch waist line. The only place I seemed to have any muscles was in my ass and thighs. For some reason I had developed a nice size and nicely shaped ass and two large thighs.

However, my sister would tell me that I had such nice looking legs for a guy. Mindy called them "girly" legs. Some of her girl friends use to tease me about my "girly" legs as well, but it was all in fun, more fun for them than me, but it was alright.

I worked out a lot over the past few years hoping to build some muscles to make up for my small size and that seemed to help but it mostly just seemed to help maintain my thighs and nice ass. The bottom line here was that I was too small to ever really considering playing profession sports.

However, I also seemed to be a good looking young fellow as I did not seem to have any problem attracting the attention of the girls. In fact, I was able to date almost any girl I wanted.

Apparently I was pretty smart also as I got almost straight "A"s in a Catholic school without much effort. Usually, I did not even have to study or do much homework, I heard the teacher explain something once and I just knew it.

I guess to be fair as I am going to tell you about the bodies of the females in this house, I should note the in addition to being short and skinny I also had a short penis. The poor thing was only about five inches long but it was pretty fat, not that that helps much, so I guess I will be no stud in the dating life as I get older. Maybe it will still grow some, but as with my height, that is just a hope and a prayer.

MINDY:

My Sister's name is Mindy, (yes, we are Mort and Mindy). Mindy was also very short, only five foot two inches tall, but she did have a nice set of full round tits and a nice plump ass. Mindy had long brown hair, a great smile, and was very nice looking. Mindy was also real smart and got good marks in school without much effort.

As with me and girls, Mindy did not seem to have any problems getting the attention of any male creatures and seemed to have her pick of any guy she wanted.

My Sister and I were real good friends and could discuss anything, even our sexual lives as they developed.

MOLLY:

My mother's best friend was Molly and she was about 38 years old and was five foot nine inches tall. Molly had medium length brown hair, small tits, nice sexy legs, and she had a nice full round ass. Molly also had a nice smile and still had a young looking face.

Molly was the mother of the twins, Ally and Cally, who, believe it or not shared the same birthday as Mindy and Me. So, we were all turned 18 that year.

Molly and her two daughters lived in a two bedroom apartment which was not in an very nice neighborhood. So, coming to live in our huge home was like hitting the lottery for them.

Molly had a full time job, but she did not have a college education, so she did not make very much money and had no opportunity to do so in the future.

ALLY:

Ally was one of the twins. Both girls had nice long sexy legs like their mom, but unlike their mom they both had nice firm round tits, not real big, but big enough to have a nice figure. They also both had nice plump asses to go along with those nice legs. They both also had beautiful long blond hair and smiles that could light up a room.

What separated the twins were their attitudes. Ally had an attitude that I think would have annoyed anyone. She was given a nice home to live in with people who were nice to her and she was always angry and uncooperative.

Ally would not clean her room, would not offer to help around the house, did not smile, did not speak nice to anyone, and Ally got poor marks in school which were getting worse.

I sort of fixed Ally thru the use of corporal punishment to make her more livable. Ally became nicer to everyone, got a little better marks, and at least kept her room clean. Ally was not a perfect kid at this point, but she was much better and has become almost tolerable.

However, Ally continued to get poor marks in school I told her that she needed to be trained as a French maid, just like Sabrina. I told Ally that if she did not want to get good enough marks to go to college then she may as well learn a trade, which was being my French maid.

Ally had to wear very short and very sexy French maid

outfits, complete with a collar and five inch high heels, just like Sabrina.

Ally looked absolutely fuckable in her French maid uniforms, but I controlled myself, I think mostly because I did not like Ally, at all, as she was so miserable.

However, even though Ally finished her high school years with all passing marks, overall, Ally's marks were not good enough to get into college.

That was until I changed everything, But, that's another story you will find out about on a Thanksgiving day on the Reform Farm.

CALLY:

When Cally first moved in with me she was a real nice kid and a pleasure to be around. However, in a short while, Molly and I both noticed that Cally was following in the footsteps of Ally and Cally's her attitude was going downhill and even her marks were slipping.

Likewise, thru the use of a couple of hard hairbrush spankings and some corner time, I straightened Cally out right away and Cally has become a nice kid to live with. I thought that Cally was much smarter than Ally and I thought she was better looking also.

Cally was also becoming my friend as she was smart enough to play a good game of chess and could talk to me about things that interested me, like science and math and finance, now, we even discuss sex a little. And, for some reason, for a lesbian, Cally enjoys giving me blow jobs sometimes, always a treat for me.

Unlike Ally, Cally accepted me as being the Boss of the house and Cally would accept her punishments as nothing more than deserved. As I said unlike Ally, who hated me for punishing her.

Thru our growing friendship, Cally, also told me things that I did not wish to hear. Cally, told me that although I was helping her, I myself, was regression into being more of a Bad Boy all the time.

When I thought about the things Cally told me, I could not say that I disagreed with her as I was not as nice of a kid as I was a year earlier. However, as I had no one to answer to, I sort of just told myself that I was having a good time so who cares about the others.

Oddly, however, I did gain respect for Cally for her courage to sort of stand up to me and try to influence me for the better. I wish I had listened to Cally, as my life would have turned out so much better if I did.

At Cally's strange request, Cally was also trained to be a French maid for the summer and she was great. Cally was a good cook, cleaned the house better then Sabrina or Ally, and served everyone with a smile all the time.

Cally also wanted to learn how to give good blow jobs and let me tell you, Cally, became a champion cock sucker. Cally seemed to be able to do whatever Cally wants to do or even says she is going to do.

Cally seems to be a really special person and has become my very good friend.

Now, I have fallen in love with Cally, the lesbian.

SABRINA:

Sabrina was my parents live in maid. I note that she was my parents maid as she did not seem to pay much attention to my needs or my room and this created a growing conflict between Sabrina and me for a number of years prior to this year.

Sabrina was about 26 years old and is a mixture of a South American Indian and black. The result made Sabrina very tall, about six foot tall, a good looking Indian with darker skin then an American Indian but not dark enough to look black.

Sabrina had very nice long and very sexy legs, a real nice muscular looking ass, medium sized tits, big enough to give her a nice figure, but nothing to say wow about. Sabrina also had a nice smile and very nice very long black hair.

I would have gotten rid of Sabrina after the funeral, but in my Moms will she asked that we keep Sabrina. Sabrina had kept my mother happy for many years since Sabrina came to be the maid when she was only 18, about 8 years ago.

I would have gotten rid of Sabrina because even though my Mom acted like Sabrina was part of the family, the fact was that Sabrina was a lousy maid. I use to complain about her all the time and the more I had to say the less and less service I got. It was like Sabrina would punish me for trying to get her to do her job better.

Anyway, my mom and Sabrina were like best friends, so

there was not much I could do, no one seemed to care about what I had to say when it came to Sabrina. Even now, my mom, was reaching back from the grave to try and protect Sabrina from me.

I loved my mom so much and we had such a great friendly and loving relationship, that I could not dismiss her request and agreed with my sister, Mindy, to keep Sabrina on, at least for a while to see if she would shape up. After all, I was now the Boss of the house, she would obey me now, NO?

TONI:

Toni, is a black girl that has become Cally loving girl friend and bed mate. Toni is not gay, as we have discovered Cally is. Rather, Toni, is bi sexual, but spends most of her sexual life with Cally. I have been invited to join them twice and both times were the best sexual experiences of my life.

Toni was about 5 foot 6 inches tall, had long straight black hair, a real nice smile, ample tits and a bigger then proportional ass, as many black girls have. Toni's ass was not fat at all, just bigger then her body frame would show as proportional. Toni had nice thighs, but overall did not have sexy legs.

Toni is a school mate of ours and was expected to die of some blood disease. However, without anyone knowing what we did, Cally and I made arrangements to donate the money Toni needed for a bone marrow transplant directly to some charity and Toni got her transplant and her life was saved and she is recovering.

Additionally, as Toni's family spent so much money trying to save Toni, before Cally and I knew of the problem, they were having their home foreclosed upon as they were not making their mortgage payments. So, Cally and I also paid off the back debt and legal fees so they could keep their home.

No one in their family knew that Cally and I were behind this mortgage payment as Cally took the money directly to the bank and paid it anonymously.

Cally asked why we were going thru so much trouble to make sure no one knew of our charity and I told her because otherwise the family and especially Toni would feel beholding to us and that was not why we were doing it. This way, they just feel some charity took care of them and they were just lucky.

I asked Cally, don't you think your relationship with Toni would be different if she knew that we spent almost $150,000.00 saving her life and bailing out her family home?

Cally recently announced that Toni was doing fine after her transplant and the doctors felt that she could make a full recovery, maybe in about six months.

I also made arrangements for Toni to continue her studies at the same university as Cally, Mindy, Ally, and now Toni. I paid for all of them, except for Mindy of course.

STEVE:

Steve is Molly's husband and Ally and Cally's father. Steve lost his job about 6 years ago and decided to become and drunk and abandon his family as he could not find another good paying job like the one he had.

This is why Molly and Ally and Cally ended up moving in with Mindy and me almost two years ago.

Anyway, I hired a private detective in California to find him.

I went to California to meet Steve after they found him to find out if he wanted to fix his life or remain a drunk forever.

He told me that he would do anything to stop drinking and get a real job and reclaim his family again. I had him sign an agreement and then the detective and a friend of his, that I also hired, followed my instructions and dried him out over the next three months.

Then I gave Steve back tThe cost to me for this Christmas gift was close to $95,000.00.

After Christmas, Cally got Steve a job and he has been doing very well and as far as we all know Steve has not touched a drink and goes to his AA meetings every week.

One week Steve missed an AA meeting and Cally brought him over to the house and strung him up in the back yard and gave him a severe whipping. Steve has not missed a meeting since that day.

THE BOSS:

The Boss is the guy who owns the Reform Farm. The Boss is a very large guy, about 6' 1" and well over 220 pounds or so and all muscle.

The Boss was a very strict man who would never tells you anything twice. You obeyed each and every command with a yes Sir or the Boss would have you severely punished. There was no half ass punishments on the Farm, just severe punishments.

However, the Boss did seem like a fair guy as he did not punish anyone just for fun or to be mean. The Boss was actually the same way I was when I would punish Sabrina or Ally or Cally. I would never punish them for fun or to be mean either, just for disobedience.

PETE AND RICK:

Pete and Rick were the Boss's Forman's and they assigned the work and made sure everybody did their jobs.

Pete and Rick were also the guys that usually punished everyone, although sometimes the Boss would also.

Pete and Rick were both very large fellows, both about 6 foot 4 inches tall and very muscular. Pete was a white guy and Rick was a black guy. They both had muscles on top of muscles and must have weighed about 240 pounds to 250 pounds compared to me at 5 foot 7 inches tall and 127 pounds.

SUMMERY:

I guess the bottom line is that because Mindy and I needed an adult to live with us for the 36 months until we turned 21, I have become the father to twin girls and a maid.

I must say that my methods have worked very well and overall, most of the time, everybody seems to get along much better and were all happier than 22 months earlier.

We all enjoyed a first successful year of college.

The Story picks up with Cally and I enjoying that weekend cruse that she bought for us.

THE CRUISE:

Cally and I left the house around 2:30 in the afternoon for the hour and a half ride to Fort Lauderdale to the port where the cruise ship departs. However, Cally seemed extra quiet during the ride. I found that to be unusual for Cally as she always seems to have plenty to talk about.

We arrived just after 4 o'clock and got to our room around 4:30 by the time we checked in and found our room. We walked around the ship for over a half hour just to see what it was like.

Then the whistle blew and we had to do this emergency exercise as what to do if the ship was sinking. That was sort of boring.

Then we sat on the balcony patio of our room and watched as the ship leave the port. That was fun as you could see things from high up in the ship that you could not see from the ground.

After we were out to sea, Cally looked at me and gave me big hug. Cally then surprised me by kissing me on the lips. Then Cally backed up a little and looked at me again and then moved back in and gave me a big French kiss. WOW! WhaI was not sure what that was all about, but I was not going to say no. Cally and I stood there making out for a few minutes. I have kissed well over a hundred different sets of lips over the past two years or so, but never a set of lips as soft and tasty as Cally's. They were best few kisses of my short life.

After those few long kisses, Cally backed away and then told me that she wanted me to taste her as well, you know like you did that one time with Sabrina. Cally even told me that she brought the chocolate sauce, as she smiled so nice, almost like she was a little embarrassed by her request.

I had no problem honoring Cally's request and if my cock was not rock hard from those kisses, I was sure it would have been hard just by Cally's request as I would have been more than happy to eat Cally's ass a long time before now.

Cally did not wait for an answer as she unhooked her sun dress and the dress just slipped down her luscious body to the floor. Cally removed her bra and I stared at her first class tits.

They were so nice and I wanted to touch them so bad, but I did not do anything until Cally told me I could as I was too afraid that Cally would change her mind and I would not get to enjoy any of her. I had no belief that I would get to enjoy all of Cally anyway, but whatever Cally was willing to offer was a bonus for me.

Cally allowed me to drink in the beauty of her body for a minute or two and then told me that since I like to remove panties so much, that I could have that privilege.

I smiled and dropped right to my knees and used my finger tips to lowered Cally's panties to the floor. That left my face level with Cally's pussy and I was just stuck in that position enjoying the view of the pussy I wanted above all others.

I looked up at Cally from my knees and I guess I was hoping Cally was going to give me permission to kiss her pussy. But, Cally, just smiled at me and turned around and told me to kiss her ass.

I thought I was going to cum in my underwear right there, right then, as I had my face right there at Cally's ass, the finest ass in all the land as far as I was concerned.

I kissed Cally's ass all over and thought it was the nicest thing that my lips had ever touched, except Cally's lips of course. I kissed Cally's ass with nice gentle kisses and then I gave Cally a few hickies and I even bit her a little.

Cally then moved away from me and laid down on the bed with her legs off the bed and I moved over between Cally's fine legs and started again.

I picked up the container of chocolate sauce off the bed and spread it all over Cally's fine ass and smeared plenty in Cally's ass crack and I used my finger to push some in Cally's ass hole too. I was in no hurry and was going to enjoy Cally's wonderful ass for a long while so I took my time licking all the sauce off of Cally's ass cheeks.

I loved being in this position, on my knees behind Cally's great looking sweet tasting ass and licking it and licking it and licking it some more. My cock was loving this so much and twitching like never before to the point where I was afraid the I was going to come in my shorts. Although what was I afraid of? That would have been delightful.

Even after I finished cleaning the sauce off Cally's ass

cheeks I still continued licking and sucking and biting Cally on the ass. Cally was responding well to my mouth making love to her ass as she squirmed and moaned and wiggled her ass real nice for me. I was enjoying myself more than I ever thought that I would. I was hoping Cally was too.

I finally stopped paying attention only to Cally's ass cheeks as I knew there were still had other parts of Cally's ass to enjoy. I lifted my head up and took a couple of deep breaths and I just dove my face into the crack of two of the greatest looking plump but firm ass cheeks I had ever seen.

I started to lick from the bottom to the top of Cally's fine ass crack. I licked along one side and then the other side and back again as I sucked up and cleaned off all of the sauce.

After a few minutes, as the top of the crack was all cleaned of the sauce, I started to work deeper, as with every third lick I used my tongue to lick deeper and deeper into Cally's crack until my tongue was all the way in and my face cheeks was firmly pressed against Cally's two soft ass cheeks. Those were really fine ass cheeks I thought and I was having a great time eating Cally's ass.

I moved my face again from Cally's ass crack to take a breath or three. Then I used my hands to spread Cally's ass cheeks a little. I moved my face back into position and started to lick Cally's ass hole.

I licked up and down and all around Cally's ass hole and I started to dart my tongue in and out of Cally's ass hole. I started to tongue fuck Cally's ass hole as well as I could and licked Cally's crack up and down and dove back in again.

Cally seemed to respond well to my efforts and was moaning and wiggling her ass real nice while saying OH! OH! OH!, YES! YES! YES!, tongue fuck me Mort, that's it tongue fuck me Mort!

I licked out all of the remaining sauce and did not miss a drop. However, like with Cally's ass cheeks, I was enjoying myself so much that when the sauce ran out I did not care and continued to tongue fuck Cally and to continued to repeat all of her previous movements only this time it was just my tongue and Cally's ass hole, but no sauce.

However, I did not care about the sauce. Cally tasted great to me, I did not need any sauce to make this an absolute thrill for me, that I was hoping to be able to enjoy many more times in the future.

Cally finally told me that it was enough and I pulled my tongue out of Cally's ass hole and lifted my face out of Cally's ass crack and took a couple of breaths and leaned back to wait and see how else I could pleasure Cally that evening.

Cally told me to get a warm towel and to clean her off. So I got up and went to the bathroom and get a nice hot towel and came back and go back down on my knees and took my good old time cleaning Cally's nice plump ass. I cleaned inside Cally's cleft and all around her anus as well.

Cally then sat up on the side of the bed and told me to stand up. Cally then unhooked my shorts and lowered my shorts and underwear to the floor and was face to cock with my piece of iron.

Cally looked at my cock and grabbed my balls ever so gently as she looked up at me and smiled and licked her lips in delight. Cally bend over and took my cock all the way in her mouth and just held it there with her nose pressed up again my belly.

Cally did not even bother to try and lubricate my cock as she sucked on it real hard and then allowed it to slowly leave her mouth. Cally then took a deep breath and licked her lips again and UMMMMM!!!! Cally took my whole cock back deep into her throat and bobbed her head up and down only a few times as Cally sucked the cum right out of me.

Cally gulped up all my cum and drank it down and not a drop escaped those luscious lips of hers. Cally kept sucking my cock slowly as she bobbed her head up and down as my cock deflated and then she allowed it to leave her mouth.

Cally looked up at me and smiled and said, UMMMM!! delicious!!!! Let's get washed up and go have dinner.

Cally and I had a lovely dinner and Cally seemed much more talkative, unlike the ride over to the port in the car. However, I still got the feeling that something else was going on in that head of Cally's, something she was not telling me, something that was bothering her.

In fact, during dinner I noticed twice that Cally was

getting a tear or two in her eye. After dinner we went to the theater and watch the show and then got some ice cream and went back to our room.

Cally held my hand for the long walk back to our room that was in the far end of the ship compared to the location of the restaurant and theater. I loved that walk, I loved holding Cally's hand, I loved being with Cally. I was falling in love with Cally.

CALLY GIVES UP HER VIRGINITY, AGAIN:

When we got back to our room after dinner and the show, without saying a word, Cally took off all her clothes and hoped up on the bed. I had a rock hard cock just from seeing Cally's naked body. She was gorgeous, one of God's best ever creations. But, it was Cally that I was finding that I loved, not her body. I had plenty of bodies before, plenty.

Cally looked over to me and told me to get undressed and patted the bed next to her. As I finished undressing and started to get on the bed, Cally looked at me and pointed to her pussy. The most beautiful and delicious pussy in the world as far as I was concerned. The only pussy that I ever thought about putting my face in.

The only pussy that I ever wanted to taste. The only pussy that I longed to taste, to lick, to kiss, to make squirm, to make explode. Yes, Cally's pussy would be a big treat and a bigger privilege. I have seen Toni enjoy Cally's pussy, but I understood that no guy has ever been near it, either with a face or a cock.

In spite of the fact that I wanted to stick my cock in Cally's pussy more than I ever wanted to stick my cock in anyone. I did as Cally told me to do, I obeyed Cally, I wanted to please Cally.

I crawled up between Cally's thighs and I was almost

to Cally's pussy when I reminded myself that I had to control my enthusiasm and not just dive my tongue right in. Rather I needed to take my time and make sure Cally has a good time.

I was reminding myself, that licking Cally's pussy was about pleasing her and not myself and if I don't remember that and do a nice job I may never get the opportunity again.

I remembered those times when I saw Toni loving Cally's pussy with her mouth and tongue and I remembered thinking about how Toni took her good old time and teased Cally and frustrated Cally before Toni finally allowed Cally to explode like nothing I ever saw before.

So, I tried to forget all about my hard cock and just thought about Cally having the night of her life, right there, right then, with a GUY! This was going to be a first for both of us.

As I have said, I have never done this before but I did watch a bunch of videos on the internet to see how it was done. In addition, as I had done when training Sabrina and Ally and even Cally to give blow jobs, I too read articles about how to eat pussy. I just never found the right girl who's pussy I wanted to put my tongue into, until now.

So, I slide my hands under Cally's thighs so I could get my hands firmly positioned, one under each ass cheek so it would be easy for me to change the pressure at certain times as I was licking and kissing and loving Cally's pussy.

I started to just use my lips by kissing gently on the inside of Cally's right thigh and then slowly used my tongue to lick up and down on the inside of Cally's very nice thighs to just below Cally's beautiful pussy lips, Cally moaned just a bit.

I did the same on Cally's left thigh and Cally wiggled just a bit. Then I started to kiss Cally again but more strongly all along the inside of Cally's thighs alternating between the right thigh and the left thigh, the left thigh and the right thigh.

Slowly I moved my mouth up towards Cally's pussy and started to kiss her pussy lips. Then I licked the outside of Cally's pussy lips, first the right side and then the left side, kissing and licking and kissing and gently licking and kissing some more while I used my hands to start squeezing Cally's ass cheeks ever so gently.

I moved to the front and inside of Cally's pussy lips and began kissing and licking and licking and kissing both the front and the inside of each pussy lip. While at the same time, I would use my hands to adjust the pressure against my mouth by squeezing tighter or relaxing my hands against Cally's ever so fine ass cheeks.

Cally was squirming and moaning a little more. I started to lick Cally's pussy lips a little stronger now and licked from the bottom to the top like an ice cream cone and pulled Cally tighter to my tongue with my hands and that got more of a reaction out of Cally as Cally started to squirm more, moan more and even moved my hips involuntary.

I kept this up for a minute or so and I kept going deeper

and deeper with my tongue with each lick until I could not get my tongue inside of Cally's pussy any deeper.

I pulled Cally even closer with my hands thereby pushing my entire face into Cally's pussy. I licked Cally a bit more while moving my head back and forth back and forth like a tiger tearing apart a piece of meat.

I started to lick around Cally's clit but did not touch it yet. I thought that I was exciting Cally and at the same time frustrating her and that was my goal, just as I saw Toni do.

All of a sudden, I guess Cally could not take any more of my teasing of her pussy and started saying NOW Mort! NOW Mort!

I immediately started licking my tongue all over Cally's clit and Cally exploded all over my face in wave after wave after wave of orgasmic delight. I could not have been happier with how my first pussy licking experience turned out. I just loved Cally's pussy, just like I thought I would.

I laid my head down on Cally's thigh and just stayed there with Cally until she was ready to move again. Cally sighed and breathed heavy and then said, Oh Mort! Oh Mort! That was great!

A couple of minutes went by and Cally whispered to me that I was time, Mort, it was time. Cally told me to slid it in and then she wanted to kiss. I rolled over on top of Cally and started to slid my cock in her extremely wet pussy, Cally's virgin pussy.

Yes, I have done many virgins before, but I never wanted to please them like I wanted to please Cally. Cally tightened up a bit as if it was hurting and I thought that it was hurting her. So, I stopped until Cally felt better and then she told me to go on.

As much as I just wanted to fuck Cally for my own pleasure. I controlled myself and stopped moving and just allowed her to get use to having my cock inside her. I just used the same theory as when I taught Cally to give blow jobs, slow and easy.

So, I stopped moving my cock and laid still and we enjoy a very nice make out session. Kissing Cally was one of my most favorite things to do, maybe my most favorite now that I thought about it. We kissed and kissed and you know what, the kisses felt different. They were better and I did not think that was possible.

After a few minutes, Cally whispered again to me to begin and I started to slid my cock in and out of Cally's hot wet pussy and within a minute I came inside Cally and she moaned like she was loving it.

I kept fucking Cally until my cock was useless as it deflated. Cally whispered to me again to use my mouth again. I slid my cock out of Cally and moved down on the bed and as I got my mouth near her pussy again I can tell you that it was one soggy mess from all of my cum and all of Cally's juices combined.

I had never eaten my own cum before, but if that's what Cally wanted, that was what I was going to do. Lick it all up Cally told me, lick it all up. I stuck out my tongue and started to lick up the combination of my own cum and Cally's sex juices.

The whole time I was working on Cally's pussy with my mouth and tongue, Cally was squirming and wiggling and moaning up a storm like I had never seen her before. I was only about half way though licking Cally clean when Cally, Now Mort, NOW!

I put my tongue back on Cally's clit and she exploded in an orgasm like I had never seen before in under a minute. I guess me just licking up all those sex juices was enough to get her almost over the edge. Cally came and came and came some more, very explosive and very long and very, very juicy.

I laid my head back down on Cally's thigh and waited until she calmed down to see if she wanted more. We must have laid there for five minutes. While we waited and I still had my head near Cally's pussy I could smell the strong scent of great sex. That was the first time I even noticed such an aroma on any girl.

I started to think that maybe it was because Cally was the first girl I ever got really excited. It most likely was, as in the past I was so selfish. I never cared about the girls, they were just my "fuck pieces". Cally, now I loved Cally and everything was totally different with her, everything.

Cally again whispered to me, I want your cock Mort, more cock. I rolled back on top of Cally and had no trouble sliding my stiff cock into Cally hot sopping wet pussy as I started to kiss Cally again.

This time however, I was kissing Cally with a mixture of pussy juices and my own cum on my lips and tongue and Cally seemed to like that and really started to moan and wiggle and kiss me more aggressively.

I was able to kiss Cally and fuck her at the same time and Cally was loving it as she moaned and kissed me back and wiggled all over the bed. This time I was able to fuck Cally for about 4 or 5 minutes before I exploded inside her again.

This time Cally grabbed my shoulders and pulled me ever so tight to her as I came. Then I realized that Cally was coming also with wave after wave after of orgasmic delight like I had never experienced before.

Cally and I just laid there bound in each other's arms for a few minutes as Cally came down off her orgasmic high. Cally then whispered to me again, lick me Mort, lick me.

Once again I moved me face back down to Cally's ever so wonderful pussy and lick up her juices as well as my own cum from Cally's pussy. Before I was finished Cally was providing me even more sex juice as she was coming once more and very violently at that.

I kept my face in Cally's pussy the whole time. This time I did not stop to put my head on her thigh, rather I just kept licking her ever so gently an Cally moaned and wiggled and moaned some more. I much have licked Cally and sucked up our fluids for over five minute before Cally tapped me on the head and told me to come here.

I moved up alongside of Cally and we hugged and cuddled and even kissed some more and then just relaxed in each other's arms.

We did not stir for about 15 or 20 minutes and then Cally whispered, thank you Mort, that was better than I ever dreamed it would be, thank you Mort.

Cally moved her hand down to my cock and found yet another rock hard cock as this evening seemed endlessly exciting to me. I had never had sex like that before, it was indescribably good, great, the best!

Cally told me to get up and I slid off the bed and just stood there. Cally moved herself over the side of the bed and put a pillow under her hips and slid her legs off the side of the bed and said, fuck me Mort, fuck me hard.

I moved over between Cally's legs and put my cock back in Cally's pussy and started to fuck her from behind as hard as I could. Cally was almost yelling in a moaning way. As she grabbed the sheets with her hands and was twisting them all up in knots.

I fucked Cally from behind like that for a good 5 or 6 minutes as she was just having the hard fucking of her life and was simply loving it. This fucking was something that Cally's pussy was loving, but that she could not get from any of her girl friends.

I filled Cally with my third deposit of hot creamy sperm that evening and then Cally whispered to me clean me Mort, clean me. I got down on my knees and kissed and licked and bit one of Gods most wonderful asses. Cally ass was like so nice to enjoy, I could not explain it to you, I could enjoy Cally's ass every day.

Anyway, I used my tongue to lick all up and down Cally's ass crack to lick out all the juices that leaked down in that area and then I even tongue fucked Cally a little and she was squirming so much my tongue kept coming out of place.

Cally whispered that was enough and she turned over and spread her legs thereby opening up her lovely pussy to me. I once again put my hot lips and hot and eager tongue to Cally's pussy and ate her to yet another orgasm.

We showered together and got back in bed and cuddled until we fell asleep.

Note: For those of you that don't pay attention, the reason this section was titled that Cally gave up her virginity a second time was because Cally offered her virginity to me when I surprised her with the present of her father after that very special Christmas, but I turned it down. So this was the second time it was offered to me.

Cally and I did not wake up the next morning until around 10 am. Even then, we just cuddled and hugged each other. I was thinking that after fucking around 115 different girls over the past 18 months, this was the first time that I actually slept with one.

We got up and were getting dressed to go to the breakfast buffet when Cally handed me a pair of black silk panties and told me to put them on. I took the panties from Cally and looked at them and then looked at Cally to object.

Cally, showed me that stern face of her and repeated, Mort, I told you to wear the panties. I smiled and just put them on. If wearing panties for Cally was going to make her happy, I sure was not going to object. It was not like anybody other then Cally and me would know about them anyway.

As we walked down the hallway and up the stairs I had to admit that the silk panties were very comfortable and felt very nice against my skin. However, I did wonder why Cally wanted me to wear the panties. I assumed that it was just because she loved it when I obeyed her. So wearing panties for her must have made her really happy.

Cally and I arrived at the buffet and like last night Cally was very quiet. I was very concerned that Cally was sorry about losing her virginity, but I was really too afraid to ask.

But then, after breakfast, we went back to our room and sat on the balcony and had some coffee as we watched the ocean float by. Cally, why last night? Cally immediately burst out in tears and started to cry so hard.

I was really feeling bad as I had to assume that Cally's distress was because of last night, after all, what else could it be? I got up and sat next to Cally on her lounge chair and put my arm around her and just hugged her while I handed her some tissues.

Cally returned the hug, so at least if she was not upset with me about losing her virginity, maybe she was upset with herself? We just sat there hugging each other for about 15 minutes before Cally finally spoke.

Mort, first, I need to tell you tHowever, I know that you are smart enough and know me well enough to know that something has been bothering me since we left the house. So, Mort, first I thank you for not pushing me into telling you what it is until I am ready. That is one of the things I really admire about you, Mort, you don't push me and you allow me to feel comfortable with whatever we do or don't do together.

Having said that Mort, I am still not ready to tell you what's bothering me. But, I will later. And Mort, when I do tell you, you will understand why I was not ready to tell you now. So, again, thank you Mort, thank you for being my friend.

However, Mort, I have a question for you, what number

am I, 130, 140, even 150? Cally, you are my first Women! Cally smiled so big she started to get tears again, but this time tears of joy and happiness. Cally? Yes Mort? Last night was the best night of my life also.

Now, Cally was crying again. I was so happy to be with Cally and to hold Cally and was happy she was sharing those tears of joy and happiness with me and no one else. Cally was the best person I had ever met.

We were docked in Key West and got off the ship and took a nice walk around the town and had some ice cream and watched some shows they had on the pier. Cally also did some shopping and I bought her a couple of nice dresses and a bathing suit.

By the time we got back on the ship it was time to shower and change and have dinner and go to the show. I enjoyed the long walk back to the room while Cally held my hand and talked to me about all sorts of things.

Cally seemed a little better, but still, there was something there that was wrong, I could feel it. But, I was not going to push Cally, she would tell me when she thought the time was right.

SATURDAY NIGHT:

That night room service delivered some chocolate milk and cookies to the room as Cally and I watched a movie in bed. As I put the milk and cookies on the night stand next to the bed, Cally pulled the sheet off herself to expose her absolutely beautiful naked body to me again.

Cally did not say anything, rather she just pointed to her pussy just like last night. Cally was high up on her bed with her head on a pillow near the headboard. I came over to the foot end of the bed so I could craw straight up between Cally's great looking legs and as I did Cally spread her legs a little to give my more room. Cally had a very nice pussy, the way I like pussies to be.

Cally's pussy was cleanly shaved with just a 4 inch high by two inch wide strip of fur above it. I thought that was so much better than a totally bald pussy area. Cally's pussy lips were so smooth and attractively shaved clean that way.

I was rock hard before I even got my face close enough to touch Cally's pussy with my lips. Just like I did last night I started to using my lips to kiss gently on the inside of Cally's thighs and then slowly used my tongue to lick up and down on the inside of Cally's very nice thighs to just below her beautiful pussy lips, Cally moaned in appreciation.

I did the same on Cally's other thigh and Cally wiggled just a bit. Then I started to kiss Cally again but more strongly all along the inside of Cally's thighs alternating between the right thigh and the left thigh, the left thigh and the right thigh.

Slowly I moved my mouth up towards Cally's pussy and started to kiss first and then lick the outside of Cally's pussy lips, first the right side and then the left side, kissing and licking and kissing and gently licking and kissing some more while I used my hands to start squeezing Cally's ass cheeks ever so gently.

I moved to the front and inside of Cally's pussy lips and began kissing and licking and licking and kissing both the front and the inside of each pussy lip while at the same time I would use my hands to adjust the pressure against my mouth by squeezing tighter or relaxing my hands against Cally's ever so fine ass cheeks.

I kept this up for a minute or so and then I started going deeper and deeper with my tongue with each lick until I could not get my tongue inside of Cally's pussy any deeper. I pulled Cally even closer with my arms thereby pushing my entire face into Cally's pussy and licked Cally a bit more while moving my head back and forth back and forth.

I started to lick around Cally's clit but did not touch it yet. I wanted tease and frustrate Cally at the same time. Then I heard, NOW Mort! do it now!

I immediately started licking my tongue all over Cally's clit and Cally exploded all over my face in wave after wave after wave. Finally Cally just nudged my head with her hand and I knew that Cally needed a break.

I laid my head on the inside of Cally's thigh and just stayed there with Cally until Cally was ready to move again. Cally sighed and breathed heavy and then said, Oh Mort! Oh Mort! That was great!

I was sort of surprised at three things. First, I seemed to be pretty good at licking Cally's pussy for her even though it was a new thing for me. Second, I was surprised as to how patient and unselfish I was with Cally as that was also something that I had never done before.

I guess the third thing I discovered was that I actually had a better time just concerning myself with pleasing Cally then I ever did only pleasing myself. That was in spite of me laying there with Cally with my cock almost hurting in frustration.

After about two minutes went by Cally calmed down and started to very lightly scratch at the pussy fur strip with her finger nails which I took as a signal that Cally was ready for another round and I went right back to work.

Like I did last night I was a little more aggressive from the start and had Cally moaning much louder this time and had Cally wiggling much more this time and I even had Cally bucking her hips more this time.

In less than two minutes as I pulled Cally real tight by pulling up on her ass cheeks and smashing my face in to Cally's pussy, Cally started another wave after wave of orgasmic delight.

Once more when Cally was finished she pushed my head away very gently and I again rested my head on Cally's thigh waiting to find out if Cally wanted another or if Cally was finished. Cally signaled me again and I went back to work for the third time and again for a fourth time before Cally was finished.

Alright Cally said, that was great Mort, just great, I'm finished now, clean me. I went to work licking up all of the juices I could with my tongue. Even during the cleanup stage I had Cally moaning and wiggling her hips a bit.

However, I was for sure thinking that after all the effort I had put in making Cally pussy purr so far that I should be able to fuck her again. But for some reason I was getting the feeling that it was not going to happen for me that evening and I was starting to feel very disappointed.

However, a few minutes later Cally held up her arms to let me know to climb on top of her and as I did I deposited my cock inside that same nice soggy pussy that I had loved with my tongue and fucked Cally ever so nice as we kissed and hugged one another until I came in under two minutes. Yes, I know, two minutes was not a long time, but I was so extra excited.

I continued to lay on Cally as my cock deflated and as it slipped out I laid to her side and we cuddled for about 10 minutes when Cally used her hand to get me hard again. I fucked Cally one more time, but this time I was able to last for about 5 minutes and we both seemed to have a great time.

I got up and got hot towel and cleaned us both and again

we cuddled and feel asleep in each other's arms. We did not even have our cookies.

We did not get up until almost 11 am as we were so cozy cuddling with each other. As I had said earlier, that was the first time for me actually sleeping with a girl and waking up with her and I was liking it very much.

We got up and showered and as we were getting dressed Cally handled me a pair of white silk panties to wear. I smiled and put them on, but did not say a word.

We went to the breakfast buffet and enjoyed our breakfast and then walked around the ship for a while to see parts that we had not previously seen before.

The ship was docked at some private island owned by the ship's company but we did not get off the ship as we live in Florida and laying on the beach or going in the ocean is something we can do all the time.

Just before 2 pm Cally told me that she made an appointment for us in the saloon for a massage and another surprise and we headed down there. Cally spoke to the lady behind the desk and another lady took me to a room and gave me a massage, which was very nice.

After she finished, another lady came into the room and uncovered me and waxed all of the hair off my groin area. I assumed that was the surprise Cally told me about. I remembered once before Cally noting that she wanted me to get waxed down there as she did not like the hair when she was given me blow jobs.

So, if Cally wanted that area hairless so she could suck my cock more often I sure had no complaint about it. Then I looked down and decided that not having the hair made my small cock look a little bigger so I even liked the idea as well.

Cally was waiting for my in the lobby after I showered to get all that oil off me and getting dressed. Cally took me over to the corner of the lobby and told me to lower my shorts and panties so she could see.

RIGHT HERE CALLY? Mort, lower you shorts and panties so I can see! I did as Cally told me to do and there were two of the workers there that could see me and watched this whole thing.

I assumed that Cally had me take my shorts and panties down just to embarrass me and I was sure embarrassed. To make things worse, as I lowered my shorts and panties together so the other ladies could not tell that I was wearing the panties, I started to get an erection.

That was the most embarrassed that I had been for a long time. Maybe the only time I was more embarrassed then that was the last two times that I got a spanking from my father when I had an erection in front of Sabrina and Mindy and my mother from being embarrassed as well.

Cally saw my new smooth shaved self down there and told me that I could pull my panties and shorts back up. However, as I did my erection was almost complete and that gave Cally a big smile. I looked over to the other two ladies and they were also smiling at me.

Cally and I took the long walk back to our room. As we were walking I realized that my cock liked those silk panties as they felt pretty good again my skin. I had an erection for almost the entire walk back to our room before it went away.

Maybe it was not the panties at all, however, maybe it was the excited feeling I got when Cally embarrassed me by making me take my pants down there in public? I was not sure. Maybe it is the feeling I am getting these days when Cally tells me what to do?

What I was sure about was that Cally was happy about the whole thing as she was smiling up a storm all the way back to the room. Whatever was on her mind for the last three days was temporarily forgotten by embarrassing me in public and having my groin waxed clean. Although, I did not think that Cally was all that happy about me getting waxed.

Rather, I thought Cally was all that happy about it because it was another step in my obeying her. My growing obedience to Cally seems to excite her greatly. For, me? Well, my growing obedience to Cally seems to excite me as well as I seem to be enjoying submitting to Cally more and more all the time.

We sat on the patio and had some ice tea and then it was time to get dressed for dinner and the show. Cally chose the Steak house that evening and we had a nice dinner and the show was a little better that night as well.

Cally held my hand for almost the entire show and sometimes she looked at me and smiled, at other times she looked like she was going to cry. I knew the hours were going by and it was soon getting to that time when she needed to tell me what was bothering her.

When we got back to our room, once again, Cally took off all her clothes and jumped up on the bed. This time however, instead of pointing to her pussy she rolled over on her tummy and put a pillow under her hips and told me to fuck her and fuck her hard.

I took off my clothes and moved up behind Cally on my knees and enjoyed feeling her ass with my hands and bent down and kissed her ass cheeks for a few minutes and then put my cock in her pussy and fucked her hard to the point where we could hear my balls slapping against Cally's pussy.

After I came, Cally turned over and I licked her to an orgasm in under two minutes. I still was not use to the taste of licking up my own cum together with Cally's pussy juices, but I got the job done anyway and Cally seemed real pleased having sex with me, "A GUY".

We also had missionary sex that night and I licked Cally to two more orgasms before she was finished for the evening.

I got a hot towel and cleaned us both and we cuddled together and fell asleep again in each other's arms.

I had fallen in love with a lesbian. Where was this going to go?

As I was falling asleep I was thinking about how much effort it was for me to please Cally and give her all those orgasms. At the same time, I was frustrated myself in being so patient.

However, I had to admit to myself that I took so much more pleasure for myself in pleasing Cally then I ever did in pleasing myself with over 100 other girls.

SO, WHAT WAS BOTHERING CALLY?

I woke up about two hours later, well after midnight. I looked over to Cally and saw Cally just laying there looking at me, with tears in her eyes, AGAIN!

Mort, let's sit on the balcony and watch the moon lit ocean while we chat. I am ready to tell you what's on my mind now.

I was happy to be sitting on the balcony with Cally, this was a great cruise I thought. It was only for the weekend, but MAN! What a weekend! The best weekend of my life and from what I could tell Cally felt the same.

Morton, I have a few things to tell you and I need for you to listen to me and not say anything until I tell you that you can speak. Morton, promise me that you will listen and let me finish and not speak until I tell you.

Wow, that was a strange request, But, sure Cally, sure.

Alright, Mort, the second thing is that I am going to have a lot of trouble getting some of this out and I may need to keep stopping to cry as I am very unhappy about what I am about to tell you. Nevertheless, just let me cry and just be patient and let me get thru this. But, Mort, do not say anything at all.

Also, Mort, you will get angry, not with me, but you will get angry and you will get upset, but I need you to promise me that you will hold yourself together. One of us crying will be enough for now. Alright Cally, I will do my best.

Alright Mort, now, when I am finished I want you to go to bed with me and just cuddle with me as you process what I am about to tell you. Then and only then are you allowed to speak, promise me Mort, promise me. Alright Cally, alright.

I could not imagine what Cally was about to tell me unless she was going somewhere and I would never see her again. I mean what else could it be. Then I started to think that maybe she was sick and was going to die and that's why we had sex. But, that would not make be angry, just sad. Just thinking about either of those two choices almost had me in tears.

Alright Mort, let's start with the last three nights. Mort, the last three nights have been the best three nights of my life. However, you questioned to me earlier was why? Why the last two nights? Why was it the right time and for the right reasons, which it most definitely was, Mort.

Mort, the reason I wanted to go on this cruise was that reason. I wanted to give you, my best friend, my virginity. I wanted to enjoy you and hope that I could enjoy having sex with a you. Mort, I wanted to have sex with you and

I wanted to find that I could enjoy it with you, which I did Mort, I loved it.

Why now, Mort? Cally started to cry again. I just waited and watched Cally cry. I wanted to hold her and comfort her, but she told me to wait until she was finished and I was going to wait. But, I felt so, so bad.

A few minutes went by, Cally continued, the reason now Mort, is because we may never have this chance again. Mort, I may not be able to see you again for a long time, maybe not ever. Mort, I wanted to be able to remember this weekend as it may be the most dear memory I may ever have of us together.

Cally burst out into tears again and I just felt so bad, so, so bad. Apparently, Cally is leaving or dying. Otherwise, what would be separating us? I again, just sat there like Cally told me to and watched her cry some more, I felt so bad, so bad. I was even getting tears in my eyes for feeling bad for Cally as I had never seen her this upset.

It must have taken Cally five minutes this time to calm down just enough to be able to speak again. Mort, Friday morning Sabrina and Ally went to the police station. I went along with them to find out what was going to happen not because I had any problem. I just went to see what they were doing because Ally told me they was going.

Mort, Sabrina and Ally filed criminal charges against you for sexual abuse. They filed charges for making them give you blow jobs and for taking them in the ass.

I was in shock!!! I did not know what to say and just sat

there and I was getting angry just as Cally told me that I would. Cally gave me a minute to digest what she just told me. Cally stopped again to wipe the tears from her eyes and blow her nose and then continued.

Mort, the bottom line here is that there is a warrant out for you arrest and that's why I took you on this cruse to get you out of the country. I made a deal with the police that you would turn yourself in when we got home tomorrow at noon time.

I was really having a problem not saying anything at this point in time, but what was I going to say anyway. So, I continued to obey Cally and I kept my mouth shut and listened.

Mort, I hired a criminal attorney who will meet you at the police station and I have arranged for bail, so you should not be in jail for more than a few hours.

After that, Mort, we will need to arrange for a plea bargain deal as you cannot afford to take this to court as you would get 25 years or more in prison for all the times you required them to service you.

Mort, I tried to stop them, but they were just too angry and I could not. However, I have spoken with the District Attorney and Sabrina and Ally about a plea deal and they are all agreeable.

The District Attorney told me that any deal that I can work out with Sabrina and Ally would most likely be alright with him as they are the victims.

However, Mort, he also told me that you would need to

go to prison for some amount of time, to be worked out later. I started to say something, but Cally held up her hand and told me that I promised, not yet Mort!

I closed my mouth. I was so angry and so afraid at the same time as this was just one big shock, I would have never thought that this was what Cally had to tell me.

Cally continued, One last thing Mort, you cannot go home as Sabrina and Ally are there. So, I arranged for a motel apartment for you to stay in pending the plea bargain and the sentencing hearing, which should take about two weeks. Then, Mort, you will be going to prison.

Cally burst into tears again and this time I did not obey her and stay put. Rather, I got up and helped her to her feet and took her to the bed and laid down with her and just hugged her and hugged her and hugged her some more.

As you could imagine, I had trouble sleeping that night. Cally fell asleep in my arms after about a hour and cried lightly almost for the entire hour. I still did not want to let her go and I think I did fall asleep about a half hour after that with Cally still in my arms.

However, I woke up again in a couple of hours and could not go back to sleep. I was shaking too much from the fear as to what was going to happen to me. All I could think about was going to prison and getting beat up and raped by a bunch of big guys. I was never so scared in my life.

I went out on the balcony and just sat and watched the

ocean go by as the sun was coming up around 6:30 that morning. About an hour later Cally was there telling me to come back to bed with her. I got back into bed with Cally and we just cuddled.

Cally started crying again and I started crying as well. I could not tell if I was more upset about going to prison or not seeing Cally again. Both, seemed equally bad to me at the time and I cried even harder.

Around 9 am we needed to eat and get off the ship, but I was not hungry. Cally went to the buffet and brought back a light snack and we ate almost nothing and just had some orange juice.

After a long silence, Cally looked at me and said Mort, yes Cally? I know the next two weeks are not going to be pleasant for you, or me for that Matter. However, I will be there for you, but I need you to do something for me as well.

Yes, Cally? Mort, I am going to be an emotional basket case. So, Mort, I need you to be the brave one. I need to be brave and take responsibility for you actions and your decisions just like you have taught me to do.

Mort, I need you to accept your punishment with honor and dignity so that I will be able to get you a better deal and get you back home to me in as short a time period as possible.

Promise me Mort, promise me that I can depend on you to hold me up thru this. Promise me I can depend on you to be my hero and get me thru this to its conclusion.

I need your strength Mort, promise me, Mort, make me proud of you.

I smiled almost, at Cally, and just said, you can depend on me Cally. I was not sure I could do as Cally asked, but I was sure going to try as Cally deserved the best I had to offer her. I was hoping I could make her proud of me, even under these circumstances.

It was a long drive back home that morning. I drove, even though Cally offered, as I thought that would help me be calmer and stronger. Cally, she was a mess, she just cried on and off thru the whole hour and a half drive, all the way to the police station, where we arrived about 15 minutes before noon time.

They took me in the back and took my picture and finger prints and filled out some forms. Then I was put in a cell by myself where I waited for about two hours and then was taken to a courtroom where my attorney told the judge I was not guilty and I was processed out on a million dollars in bail.

Cally, as she told me before, had already made the arrangements for the trust banker to put up the million dollars as collateral. My attorney noted that he expected a plea agreement and would like to schedule the sentencing hearing.

Everyone agreed to June 27th, only seven days away.

Cally came back with me to my hotel and we sat around looking at one another for a while. Cally, I don't know what to say. Molly and Mindy warned me and I paid no attention to them.

I only stopped doing it when you told me to, Cally, at least I obeyed you, but I guess that was too late.

Cally, if you have something else you could be doing, maybe you should go and do it and come back later. Right now I will not be very good company.

So, Cally left and I just laid on the bed and cried a little and worried a whole lot and got more and more scared as time went along.

Cally came back the evening and we watched the news together and just held each other and finally got some sleep.

PLEA BARGAIN:

Cally and I went to my attorney's office to discuss my options. Cally told us that she thinks that she has already work out a deal the Sabrina and Ally would agree to, but they just wanted to think about it for a day or two.

What Cally presented to me was this; Both Sabrina and Ally agreed that 10 years in prison was enough punishment to satisfy them. As you can imagine going to prison was the absolutely last choice in a plea bargain for most people and it certainly was for me. 10 years sounded like a long time to me.

Anyway, Cally offered instead of 10 years in prison, I was to be sent to a work farm, called the REFORM FARM about an hour ride from my house, for only 4 years.

The work farm would have complete control over me for those four years. They could keep me on the farm, they could let me go home and supervise me, they could let me out on a work release project, they could let me manage the work farm, basically anything they decided.

They could even decide that I could not learn to behave and send me to prison for what was left of the ten years, it was all up to them. If at the end of 4 years I had met all of their requirements, then I would be free for good. I did not even need to be on parole, I would just be free.

However, I needed to sign a consent contract acknowledging that I fully understood that corporal punishments were used on the farm and I would agreed that I would accept such corporal punishments, including spankings, canings, strapping's, and even a whipping.

There was a lot more to the agreement but I did not read it as Cally never gave it to me, she just told me about the highlights. As you can imagine I thought it was fine for me to had given Sabrina and Ally and Cally those same type of punishments, but I did not think it was not alright for me to have to endure them.

I guess I was really still refusing to admit that I did anything wrong and therefore I did not deserve any punishment. Well, maybe I was just scared and afraid to make a decision. So, I was holding up the plea bargain as I just could not seem to agree to anything.

Like Ally and Sabrina, I said that I wanted to think about it and would decide later. However, time was running out and I still did not agree.

On the third night, Cally came and spent the night with me again. We did not have sex or anything. I was not in the mood any more than Cally was. Cally was first and foremost my friend and that's what I needed right then and that's what I got from Cally, my friend, my loving friend, Cally.

Cally told me that Sabrina and Ally agreed to the plea deal. Cally told me that in the beginning Sabrina and Ally just wanted me in prison for as long as I could be kept there. However she convinced them to agree to the deal because it makes no sense just to punish me and not get anything for themselves other then emotional satisfaction.

So, Cally told me, Mort, the real truth here is that I do not want you to have to go to prison for ten years. I have negotiated a deal for everyone, where everyone gets a good deal, to an understandable degree and everyone gives up parts of what they wanted. I believe it is the best deal that I could get for you and still keep them happy.

So here is the bottom line Mort, I do not think you will get a better deal than this one, unless you really think that some jury is going to think that what you were doing was alright and I know you are smart enough to know that would not happen.

So, if for no other reason Mort, I, Cally, want you to take the deal for me. I don't want to see you punished any more than is necessary. I believe under this deal Sabrina and Ally will be able to overcome their emotional hatred for you and shame for themselves.

As well, I believe that you will be sufficiently punished to the point where you will come to agree that you were properly punished and then we can move on in life.

I had no idea why Cally still cared about me, but she seemed to. I had no idea what Cally meant by then "we can move on in life" but then most the time Cally tells me things she is the only one of us that understands what she means and I am just left wondering what she meant.

As I was thinking and enjoying Cally's beauty, especially

the peak at those nice breast that Cally seemed so proud to show off to me, Cally interrupted me.

Cally looked at me like she never looked at me before, like she really cared about me and said. Mort, I am telling you right here right now to accept the deal.

Mort, I am telling you right here and right now that I want you to be brave for "ME" and accept the deal because I am telling you to! Mort, I am telling you to obey me, NOW! I still remained quiet as I was having way to much trouble agreeing to anything that I did not like.

Mort, I really don't care at this point what you think of it, I just want you to sign it, if for no other reason than because I am telling you to. Mort, that should be a good enough reason for you after what you have done and after what you are putting me though. Cally never spoke to me like that before, both stern and loving at the same time.

Then I noticed the strangest thing, I got an instant boner. I did not get an erection from Cally's pretty face, or her nice tits, or her great looking legs, or even that fine ass of hers that day. I got an erection from her stern attitude with me as she was basically telling me what to do.

I just looked at Cally and was about to say something. MORT, SAY NOTHING AND SIGN THE PAPER! MORT, OBEY ME AND OBEY ME NOW, I DON'T WANT TO HEAR ANOTHER WORD FROM YOU ABOUT IT! As much as I wanted to, I just could not disobey her and said, fine Cally.

Cally got up and with a big smile on her face came over to me and gave me one of the best kisses of our lives.

Cally has never told me that she loves me, and in fact, I have never told her that I loved her. However, she is sure behaving like she loves me by what she has done for me, how she has treated me, and what she has said to me.

However, as apparently I am going away to the REFORM FARM for 4 years I guess it is not an issue right now.

Alright, Mort, here is the rest of the deal, the main reason that Ally and Sabrina agreed to this deal.

Everyone, including, Ally, Sabrina, Molly, and myself, get to remain living in your house free of charge for those four years. Sabrina would remain the houses maid.

Additionally, as you have already agreed, you will continue to pay for college for Ally and me.

Fair enough Mort? Sure Cally, that's fine with me, I was not going to make you leave anyway and I was not going to withhold any college money that I already promised to anyone.

Cally gave me a big smile and, I know Mort, I knew you would say that.

Alright, Mort, that is the end of the plea agreement, Sabrina and Ally have already signed off on their end, I just need you to sign her for me Mort. I signed.

Alright, Mort, one more thing and this is for me and it is all my idea. I would like to build a new house for us on the river in Fort Myers so we can have a house of our own when you get out.

I was stunned! Cally never stops surprising me. Cally was acting like we were married, what did she mean, "a house of our own"?

Well, it did not take me long to say yes because anything that would keep Cally with me under any circumstance was more than alright with me. Hell, I would give Cally a house if it meant that I got Cally as part of the deal, sign me up I thought.

Cally gave me one of her big smiles that just lights up the room and told me that she would get an architect to design some samples and show them to me next month.

Cally and I talked about other things after that for over two hours, including the plans for a new house that we would build. Cally went out and got us some dinner and stayed the night and held my hand and cuddled me until I fell asleep.

The next morning, Cally told me that she had things to do and she would call me later.

It was a long weekend for me in the hotel room. I was allowed to go out, but I just did not feel like it. Cally spent most of the weekend with me and I sort of hinted that I would like to have sex.

However, Cally told me that she had such a great time on the cruise for those three nights and those three nights are the three nights that she needs to remember for the next four years. You can't improve upon perfection Cally said, so, Mort, I need to have my memories.

I sure could not argue with Cally. If that was the way she felt, I sure understood it. In fact, those perfect memories may be all I have to remember Cally for forever, as there is no guarantee that I will ever enjoy her again after my four years is up.

The morning of the sentencing hearing Cally and I had nice breakfast together and then Cally told me that she needed to speak with me before we left.

First Mort, I am not sure how this works, if they take you away today, these will be our last moments together so I need to say some things to you now as I may not get the chance later.

Ok Mort, First, when you are standing there in front of the judge, he will be looking at you to see if you are ready to admit you were wrong and that you have remorse for your crimes, very important that the judge hears you say that and feels that you mean it.

Don't forget, Mort, the judge is not required to agree to this deal and then things could get much worse from there.

So, Mort, this is what I want you to do;

One, You are to stand up straight and look directly at the judge,

Two, you need to freely admit to what you have done,

Three, you need to freely admit that you are sorry and ashamed of   yourself.

Four, you need to freely admit that you are there to be punished   and that you deserve to be punished.

Five, if all else fails, Mort, I want to be proud of you when I leave that court room today.

Mort, I know you will obey me, however, tell me that you will make me proud of you, it will make me feel better as the tears were starting to flow down Cally's cheeks.

I will Cally, I will make you proud of me today. I was sure hoping that I could keep that promise.

Cally drove me to the sentencing hearing as I was too nervous to drive. I was so upset and so nervous my legs were shaking and I was having trouble even walking.

I got out of the car and Cally came around and took my hand and held my hand all the way to the courtroom where she sat me down. I just stayed put until the proceedings started.

The sentencing hearing was going to be the end of me not knowing how long I was going to prison and the beginning of me going to prison. I thought I was going to be sick. Cally got me a bottle of water and sat down next to me and told me to look at her.

I looked into Cally beautiful eyes and Cally told me, Mort, listen to me. I know this is hard and I am not pretending it is not. But, I want you to say what I told you to say and I want you to be brave for me today. Understand Mort? Yes Cally.

Within the next 10 minutes, Ally, Sabrina, the District

attorney, and my attorney all showed up. Just a few minutes later the bailiff announced the Judges name and we all stood up as the judge entered and sat down.

My tummy started doing flip flops and my legs were shaking uncontrollably. Cally could feel me and took my hand and held it tight. I tried to smile to Cally, but my mouth did not work very well.

The Judge sat down and asked everybody if they were ready and both attorneys said yes your honor and we all sat down.

The judge looked at the district attorney and told him that he read his half page sentencing report. Jack, it was a half page, it had no information in it about the boy. All you said was, what he did and nail him to the wall, you should be ashamed of yourself, sit down Jack.

The judge looked at my attorney and said, Peter, you sentencing recommendation is only one page in length, yes twice as long as Jack's but does not say anything other than, he's a good kid who made youthful mistakes and I should cut him a break. You too, Peter, should be ashamed of yourself, sit down Peter.

The judge then said, now, I have a third sentencing report. However, this report is titled instructions and not recommendations.

Nevertheless, The judge said that he read the 11 page pre sentencing report which titled "The Judges Sentencing INSTRUCTIONS". Who is this Cally person who wrote this "Instructional manual" for me?

Cally, who was sitting next to me stood up and told the judge that she was Cally. Really, the judge said?

I was wondering why Cally was the issue here, and it did not sound like the judge was happy with her, as apparently Cally was trying to tell the judge what to do and he was not taking it so kindly. How that was helping me, I was not sure.

Cally, who are you to the defendant? Just his friend, Sir. Just a friend Cally, not his wife, no Sir, your honor. Cally, are you his girlfriend? No Sir, your honor, just his best friend.

Well, let me tell you something MISS CALLY! OH! MY! This did not sound good for me, Cally was pissing off the judge. Cally, I have been a judge for over 30 years now and have read hundreds of pre sentencing reports and this is by far the best one I have ever read. I congratulate you, Miss Cally. You sure showed these two attorneys a thing or two.

Well, I guess that went well after all. However, Cally, the judge continued, if you ever do anything like this again, you may wish to call it a sentencing recommendation report instead of a sentencing instruction report.

Judges like me don't take kindly to being told what to do, understand, Miss Cally? Yes Your honor. Good Cally, please sit down and we will continue.

Morton, please stand up. I did. Tell me why we are here today Morton? Your honor, We are all here today because I forgot what my father tried to teach me for the first 18 years of my life.

Your honor, my father taught me;

To always be polite to everyone, all the time, no matter what. However, I failed to obey that rule and was not polite to Sabrina and Ally and many others.

My father taught me to always be friendly and nice to everyone, all the time. However, I failed to obey that rule as I was not so friendly to Sabrina and Ally, and many others.

My father taught me to do the right thing, even when it's hard to do the right thing. However, I failed to obey that rule as well and did not do the right thing with Sabrina and Ally and others was well.

My father taught me not to gamble, yet I gambled.

My father taught me to be honest with myself and others. However, I lied to myself and I was not honest with others.

My father taught me that whatever I do, I should always be proud of myself. Your honor, I disobeyed my father as I am not proud of myself. In fact, I have never been more ashamed of anybody in my whole life then I am of myself at this time.

Your Honor, you see that unhappy crying face? Yes son, I do see Cally's face. How can I even overcome my shame to the degree that I can make that face right. My shame in front of Cally is the heaviest burden I could ever imagine carrying.

Your honor, I can only hope that I can find a way to make

amends to those that I hurt in some way, some day. That would be the only way to remove the pain that I caused and to lessen my own shame and take steps towards fixing that face that Cally now has because of me.

Therefore, your honor, we are all here today to decide on my punishment as I have been a Bad Boy, a real Bad boy and your honor, no one deserves to be punished for their actions more than I do. However, your honor, that will only be the beginning of a long road to try and make things right, or at least, as right as they can be.

The judge just looked at me and stared, sort of like he did not know what to say. Cally started crying and held her hands over her face and just cried and cried.

I was just hoping that Cally's tears were tears of pride as all I wanted to do this day was make Cally proud of me. Making Cally proud of me was all I had to give her at this point in time and I wanted her to have the gift she asked for, no matter what. I tried to honestly do that with that statement.

So, Morton, you're telling me how you treat those two beautiful young girls was wrong. Yes Your honor. So, why did you treat them that way, son? I was a just a Bad Boy, your honor, I make no excuses for my poor behavior.

So, Morton, did you come to this realization on your own one day? No your honor, I learned it through my relationship with Cally.

Alright Morton that's good start. Morton, according to this report that your friend Cally wrote, it says that you routinely, over a period of about 14 months required Ally to give you blow jobs on demand. Is that true, Son?

Yes Sir, your honor. Son, are you aware that I could send you to prison for 25 years for that crime alone? I had trouble saying anything as my mouth did not seem to be working any longer.

Cally moved closer to me and took my hand and squeezed it hard and I choked out a yes, your honor. The judge noticed what Cally did and sort of nodded his head in approval.

Alright son, then it say here that you also would have anal sex with Ally whenever you wanted to as well, is that true? Yes your honor. Are you also aware that I could sentence you to 25 years in prison alone for that crime, son? Again, I was so nervous I was having trouble just standing up. Cally again squeezed my hand and I said yes Sir.

Then it says in here that about 8 months ago at Thanksgiving that you just stopped and never bothered Ally again. Why was that, Son? I had trouble speaking as my legs were shaking so badly and I still felt like throwing up.

You honor, I stopped because Cally told me to. Really, son? It says here that Cally told you, and I quote, "that I want you to stop putting you dick in my sister". Is that what Cally told you son? Yes your honor, as I looked to Cally and tried to smile, but my lips were not cooperating.

So, son, Cally just told you to stop putting your dick in

her sister and you just simply obey her, and that's it? Yes your honor. Interesting, the judge commented.

Alright, son, we are up to 50 years so far, but let's move on. It says here that you also used Sabrina for blow jobs anytime you wanted on which was several time a month. Is that true also, son? Yes your honor, alright, so now we are up to 75 years.

Finally son, you also used Sabrina to have anal sex with on demand over that same period of time, is that true son? Yes your honor. Alright son, I guess we are finished and we are up to 100 years.

Now, son, it also says here that you stopped using Sabrina about 6 months ago, true son? Yes Your honor. And why was that? Because Cally told me to, Sir. Yes, that's what it says in this report and I quote, "I do not what you porking Sabrina any more, it is not the right thing to do".

Is that what Cally told you son? Yes your honor. And that's all it took for you to stop abusing Sabrina? Yes Sir. But, Cally is not your girlfriend and you are not sleeping with her, she is just a friend, your best friend, is that what you what me to believe son? Yes Your honor.

Alright son, you have my attention, so why do you obey Cally, what the connection here, son? I really don't know your honor. Cally is just an extraordinary person and she is my best friend and for some reason I cannot explain, I just obey her, Sir.

Interesting, very interesting son. I don't get that, but for now we will leave it alone. However, I would like to discuss the remorse issue. I understand that you stopped "putting your dick in her sister" and that you "stopped porking Sabrina" because Cally told you to, but did you think what you were doing was wrong, son?

No, your honor, I always thought that they could leave if they did not like it and therefore it was voluntary on their part. Alright son I can understand your thinking, so when and why did you decide that you had done something wrong?

Your honor, when Cally told me that I needed to stop using Ally and Sabrina, she offered herself as a substitute. Cally told me that she would give me all the blow jobs I wanted if I stopped using Ally and Sabrina.

Really son, interesting, so have you been using Cally instead, I did not see that in the report Cally wrote? No Sir, I have not used Cally, not even once. Really son, tell me why?

Well, your honor, that's the point here. I just never felt right about using Cally for anything. Cally deserved my respect and my friendship and I just could not use her that way.

So, you honor, that's when I realized that it was also wrong to use Ally and Sabrina, but that I just did not care because I did not like them. So, I lied to myself and told myself that it was alright.

Then your honor, Cally sealed my guilt for me when she told me that from that day forward she wanted me to behave, always, in a manner which would make her proud of me as she had made me proud of her.

You honor, that's when it really hit me that I was not proud of myself any longer. Ever since that day, I have made each and every day of my life a point to make Cally proud of me. Hence, my Bad Boy behavior was behind me.

Today you honor, I stand here to accept my punishment in the best manner I can to make Cally proud of me.

At this point, there was another break while both Cally and I cried together, maybe for the last time.

Cally, stand up please, yes your honor. Is this true, you offered yourself as an alternative plaything to Mort. Yes, your honor. So, Cally, it would have been alright that he used you? No, your honor.

Cally, I'm confused? Your honor, I did offer myself as an alternative plaything, as you say, because I knew Morton would not accept my offer, but then, he would have no excuse to continue to use Ally or Sabrina.

Cally, that is some chance you took, how did you know he would not use you? Your honor, I took no chance, that's my whole point here today, I knew Morton was a very good person deep down inside and I just knew he would not use me.

Alright Cally, has Morton made you proud of him since then, As Cally started to cry again, she spurted out, YES YOUR HONOR, EVERYDAY!

Alright, Cally, you may sit down and we will move on to some sentence questions. You can sit down too son, I will get back to you.

Ally, please stand up. As Ally stood up, the judge said, Ally, I understand that you have agreed to this sentencing "ORDER" that Cally wrote for me? Yes Sir. Ally you don't sound all that happy about it? No Sir. Then why are you agreeing to it, Ally? Your honor, Cally told me to agree to it.

Really Ally? Yes Sir. Alright Ally, so why are you obeying Cally? Sir, I am not sure, I just do! Cally always seems to know what the right thing to do is. The judge smiled and laughed a little. You can sit down Ally, thank you your honor.

Sabrina, please stand up. Yes Sir. Sabrina, have you agreed to this sentence "ORDER"? Sabrina was quiet and said nothing for about 15 seconds. Then all that was heard in the courtroom was Cally voice, in a loud and authoritative voice say, SABRINA!

Yes Sir, I agreed to the sentencing order, your honor, Sabrina said. The judge looked at Cally and then looked at Sabrina and then asked Sabrina, Sabrina are you also only agreeing to this order because Cally has told you to? Yes Sir.

Alright Sabrina, and why do you obey Cally? I could not tell you, your honor, there is just something special about Cally and when she tells you what to do, you just do it.

Well, as the judge looked over to Cally and told everyone that in over 30 years on the bench this is the most interesting case he has ever had. Nevertheless, we are starting with 100 years in prison and let's see where we go from here.

Morton please stand up, yes Sir. It says here in this report that everyone has agreed to 10 years in prison or 4 years on the REFORM FARM. Morton, do you know what happens on the prison farm and how you will be treated there?

No Sir, NO? No Sir, then Morton, why did you sign this agreement not knowing what was going to happen to you? NO! NO! Morton, don't tell me, let me guess. Because Cally told you too? I almost smiled when I replied, that is correct your honor, because Cally told me too.

Cally, please stand up, yes Sir. Cally, you apparently negotiated this deal for Morton without his knowledge, correct? Yes your honor. Cally, don't you think he has a right to know what he is in for on that prison farm?

Your honor, Mort spent 18 months getting himself into this mess and I decided that the shorter prison farm sentence was at least as punishing as 10 years in a real prison. I decided that I wanted him to be punished in that manner as it was more akin to how he treated Ally and Sabrina.

Also, your honor, I wanted Mort to be able to come back to me as soon as possible. I wanted Mort to come back to me well punished and ready to be a good citizen and ready to again be my best friend for the rest of his life, your honor.

Cally, come on, again, this guy is not your boyfriend and you are looking out for him and making decisions about his life like this, why? Your honor, Mort could be a very special person, he's bright, he's very generous, and is very caring young man.

Your honor, Mort, just lost himself there for a while and needs to be punished and punished severely for what he did, but he does not need to have his life taken from him.

You honor, as Cally started to cry again, Mort is my best friend in this world and has done more for me and my family in those same months than anyone could ever expect from another person in a entire lifetime and I want him back! He deserves to be given back to me and I feel that I deserve to get him back.

Cally, just as a side question. How do you think that your sister Ally feels about you being on Morton's side of this issue instead of supporting your sister?

Your honor, I love my sister and we are good friends. While it is true that I wish to help Mort in this matter, I am not against me sister, Ally. Both Ally and I agree that Morton should be punished.

Now, your honor, it's just a matter of how long he will be punished and we have no argument with one another over that issue. Ally is agreeable with my thoughts on the sentencing. Ally and I will be home later today being the same good friends that we have always been. Aright Cally, please sit down, yes your honor.

Is there a Steve in the courtroom? Yes Sir, as Steve stood up. Steve, I understand that you hate Morton and wish that he rots in jail for the rest of his life. Yes, your honor.

Steve, is it not true that you decided that it was in the best interest of your loving wife of 13 years and your two twin girls of 13 years that you become a drunk and abandon them. Well, your honor, that's not exactly what I decided. But, Steve, is that not what happened, yes your honor.

So, Steve, after you abandoned your family is it not true that Morton took care of them, gave them a nice home to live in, got them an education, and bought them nice clothes, computers, cell phones, fed them, and is now paying for them to go to college? Yes, your honor.

Alright Steve, is it not true that with his own money Mort hired a detective to find you? Yes, your honor. Then is it not true that Morton paid a doctor and another man to dry you out and return you to your family? Yes, your honor.

Then is it not true that Morton gave you the money to rent and furnish an apartment so you could stay close to the family that you abandoned? Yes, your honor.

Steve, have you had a drink in the last 9 months since Morton took over control of your life, no your honor. Steve don't you think that this is a remarkable thing for some 19 year old boy to do, don't you feel that Morton gave you your life and your family back?

Yes, your honor, Morton gave me my life back and then Morton gave me my family back as well. So. Steve, when was the last time you had a drink? Your honor, it was 8 months, 17 days ago. Congratulations Steve, I know that's a tough achievement. Do you think you can continue, Steve?

Your honor, I have Cally watching my every move, so, yes, your honor. The judge smiled and laughed a little and looked over at Cally and said, yes Steve, I can see how that would work for you. However, Steve, that does not explain how you can hate someone who gave you your life back and then gave you your family back?

Your honor, I just hated the way he went about the process. OH! I see, Steve, even though Morton's method worked, you did not like it and in spite of all the other things he has done for you and your family, you sit in judgment of him because you did not enjoy the process. I think I have the picture, Steve, I think you should be ashamed of yourself. Steve, you can sit down. Thank you, your honor.

Mort, I also see a note in this report about a Toni and a bone marrow transplant. Are you related to Toni in some way? No your honor. Yet, you paid $13,000.00 so Toni's family would not lose their home to foreclosure and paid somewhere in the neighborhood or $150,000.00 for the bone marrow transplant and Toni's other medical needs to save her life? Yes your honor.

Why? Your honor, Toni is a good friend of Cally's, so we helped save her life and we helped out her family also. There is nothing more to it than that, your honor. The judge just looked at me for a minute and then said, Alright, I don't get that either, but there is a lot going on here today that I don't understand, so let's move on.

Cally, anything else? Your honor, I know you read the rest of my report noting all the good parts of Mort. Yes

Cally, I have, you may sit down and I will give you my decision, thank you, your honor.

However, before I do, I have a few things to say. First, I wish to say that I am very sorry to Sabrina and Ally as no lady should have had to go thru what happened to you two.

Second, even though you two were reluctant to agree to this deal, let me assure you that you will be much more satisfied that Morton has been punished thru the prison farm where you can go and see him be punished then if he went to a regular prison where you may never see him again. The prison farm will satisfy your desire for revenge much better, you wait and see.

Morton, please stand up, yes Sir. Morton, in most cases like this I usually sentence the violators to up to 25 years in prison. However, in your case, which I noted before is the most unusual case I have ever had.

First, Morton, I do recognize that all you crimes were performed when you were "young and stupid" as Cally points out in her "ORDER" to me.

Second, Morton, it is such a rare case when the criminal corrects his own life and stops being a criminal before he gets caught. That says volumes about your potential character, again, as Cally points out in her "ORDER" to me.

Third, I have never had a case like this where the defendant, who has been both terribly bad and so extra good at the same time. Let's be honest here Sabrina and Ally, Morton has done more good in the last two years than most people do in a life time and much of it to the benefit of you two and your families.

Fourth, Morton, I cannot remember in my 30 years or so on this bench, a young man coming before me that stood here as you have today and freely admitted his crimes, made no excuses for himself, and was so willing to accept his punishment, as you have done today.

Your brutal honesty in this courtroom and the courage it took to stand before me as you have done today, has moved me. That together with some of the other things Cally wrote in her "ORDER" makes me believe that Cally is correct and there is a good person in you and that you should be saved from a life time of prison.

Nevertheless, Morton you have been a Bad Boy, a real Bad Boy and need to be punished. As for Cally and her "ORDER"? I see for some reason that everyone in this group seems to obeys Cally, even though they are not sure why.

So, Morton, for the first time in my life as a judge, as I am going to obey Cally too. Morton, you are hereby sentenced to 10 years in prison or 4 years on the prison farm, your choice, Morton.

I could not tell if I was happy, relieved, or unhappy that I was going to jail. But, Cally was real happy and that made me feel somewhat better.

Cally, you stay close to Morton through his upcoming ordeal, he is going to need your strength to get through it.

Three more things Morton! Yes Sir. One, don't ever come back here again! I will not be so nice the second time around. Second, don't ever give up Cally. I agree with you that she is a remarkable young women and friend. In addition to your own courage in this courtroom today, you can thank her that you did not get 25 years in prison.

Third, Cally points out in her order that part of the agreement is that you are not to be put on the sex offenders registry and to have your file sealed once you complete you sentence.

Cally, before I give you my decision on this issue, I have one more question for you. Did you give Morton any advice for today? Yes, your honor, I told Mort that I wanted him to make me proud.

Cally, that was good advice. How do you think he did? Cally just burst out in tears and could not answer. I looked at Cally and started to cry again as well.

The judge smiled at Cally and just said, I agree Cally, I agree.

The judge sat patiently until Cally got herself under control and the said. Cally, I struggled with this case due to the ongoing extensive sexual crimes involved. However, Cally, because of all the remarkable parts of Morton's life, I will also obey you in this matter. I agree with you and I think Morton has earned that right and I so order his record to be sealed and he not be placed on the sex offender registry.

Last, is there any comments on the incarceration date?

Your honor? Yes son? Your honor, would July 1st be alright, I have a few things that I could use a day or two to handle? Sure, son, July 1st will be fine noon time. See the bailiff and he will give you the directions.

Good luck to you son!

We are finish here, BANG! went the gavel and the judge left.

Cally and I left the courtroom together and drove back to my hotel. Cally wanted to talk about what just happened and I told Cally that I wanted to go and see my trust banker and think about what just happened and then speak with her later.

Cally told me that was fine and she left to go home and to see how everyone there was feeling about the conclusion to this unhappy affair. I asked Cally to bring Mindy back and the three of us would have dinner together.

Mindy followed Cally back to the hotel and we had dinner together in the hotel. I did not have much to say to Mindy except to apologize to her for any embarrassment and or the shame that I brought upon the family.

I told Mindy that I too wished I had listened to her when she warned me about becoming a Bad Boy. Additionally, I told Mindy that Molly told me the same thing and I did not listen to her either. In fact, Cally told me the same thing and I ignore her good advice as well. So, Mindy, I brought this upon myself and I will just have to pay the price.

As Mindy was leaving, she gave me a nice hug and wished me luck and told me she loved me as she started to tear up. I also got a few tears in my eyes and told her that I loved her too.

After Mindy left, I gave Cally a credit card that I got from the trust banker that afternoon. I told Cally to use the credit card for anything that everybody needs for school and for anything else she needs for the house or for herself.

Cally, smiled at me and asked if I trust her that much? Cally, As I was getting tears in my eyes, I trust you more than anyone and I want to make sure you have everything you need for the next four years so you do not need to concern yourself with anything other than then finishing your education.

Also, Cally, here is another credit card for Ally. Ally's card only has a $1000.00 credit limit on it. That should be enough for her to pay for anything she needs each month. If she needs something else, she will need to ask you.

Cally and I went back to my room and Cally asked me to tell her about how I was feeling about the sentencing hearing.

Well, Cally, I am glad it's over, at least I know what's going to happen to me and 4 years is a lot better than 25 years, by far.

However, Cally, did I make you proud of me? Cally burst into tears and I did too in response to Cally's crying. Cally grabbed me and hugged me so hard. We hugged and cried together for a couple of minutes. As she calmed down, Cally told me, yes Mort, more that she could ever have imagined.

Cally, I need to thank you for this farm deal. Working

on a farm has to be better than being in prison, even if it is hard work. Work will not hurt me and it may help pass the time better.

Both Cally and I were really tired and we went to bed. I really wanted to have sex with Cally, but I guess she was not in the right frame of mind. However, Cally did give me a nice blow job and I fell right to sleep.

THE NEXT DAY:

Both Cally and I got a good night's sleep, the first one in three nights. So, I guess that meant that we have both accepted what was going to happen and where I was going to go.

As Cally and I were having breakfast the next morning I told Cally that I needed to go to her college and make some arrangements to make sure that everything gets paid for automatically thru the trust so she did not need to worry about the tuition.

I asked Cally to go to the house and get my computer, my DVR, and my flat screen TV from my bedroom. I also asked Cally to get some clothes for me. Some shorts, underwear, shirts and one pair of shoes and some long pants with a belt.

I told Cally that I would meet her back at the hotel for dinner as I thought it would take me all day. I Also asked Cally to bring Molly to dinner that night so I could say goodbye to her. Cally agreed to everything and told me that Toni was coming home from New York that day and she would go and see how she was doing.

Cally met me back at the hotel with Molly and we had dinner together. I told Molly that I was very sorry for all the pain I had cause her and that I wished I was smart enough to take her advice as we would not be having this discussion if I had.

Molly, I also wish to tell you that I have no animosity towards Ally and Sabrina for having me arrested as I cannot blame them, I can only blame myself.

Accordingly, I have full intentions to make sure that all three of you have everything you need for the next four years. Molly, here is a credit card for you to use while I am gone.

You are welcome to use it for anything that you need for the house, or if an emergency come up. If anything serious happens then talk with Cally as she will have additional funds available to her also.

Cally told us that she went to see Toni and Toni was doing well, but very weak from all the chemotherapy and or radiation treatments. However, the doctors told her that she was doing very well and should recover enough strength for her to go back to college in September.

That's the good news Mort. However, the bad news is that Toni was too sick to get her application in for college aid in time. Additionally, as she was not able to the last semester she had lost her loan and now has no money to go to college.

I smiled at Cally and gave Cally yet another credit card. Another one Mort? Yes Cally, this one is to be used for all the college needs for Toni. Toni? Mort? did you not just hear me about Toni not going to college?

Cally, Toni will be getting a letter from the same college you are going to, telling her that there were a few extra openings and that she has been accepted to that university and that she has received a grant from a local charity that helped her out due to her condition.

Cally looked at me, looked at Molly, looked at me, and they both started to cry a little. How Mort, How did you do that? Cally, I did not do anything wrong, I just talked the dean into it while I was there paying for yours and Ally's tuition today.

So, I also paid for Toni's tuition as well. Mort, that was so nice of you, Cally said, I do not know what to say? Molly started crying even harder and Cally and I just watched her cry as I handed her an extra napkin to wipe her eyes.

After Molly left, I told Cally that there was one more thing I wanted to speak with her about. Yes, Mort? Cally, I think it would be a good idea for you to have Toni move in with you.

Cally, you would have more company without me being there and you would be able to help her with her college work. And, most important, Cally, you would be able to make sure that she is getting all the follow up medical help that she needs for the next year or so until she is completely better.

Also, Cally, I would like you to clean out everything in my room and give everything away to the homeless shelter and you should move into my room and give Toni yours.

Mort, STOP TALKING! Mort, I am not sure what is going on here. My sister, Ally, is having you sent to prison and you asked the judge to give you two days so you can make sure everyone in my family, including Ally, is taken care of, in addition to Toni.

Am I missing something Mort, how can you be so nice and thoughtful and loving under these circumstances? I just don't know what to say, Mort. You are treating me like a queen and I am just overwhelmed with joy and appreciation.

Cally, I am trying to do the right thing here, the things that would make you and me both proud of me. I have let us both down and this is my beginning to try and fix things.

Alright, Cally, I think I have covered everything. Will you stay with me again tonight. Mort, you could not stop me.

Cally and I went back to my room and I figured I had nothing to lose by asking at this point, so I went over to Cally and hugged her and gave her a nice kiss and asked her if we could have sex this last time?

Cally started to take off her clothes and by the time I was naked I already had a raging erection. Cally likes looking at my cock, she even moved over and grabbed it with her hand and felt my balls and played with my cock for a minute or two.

Cally laid on the bed and I climbed on top of her and she told me just fuck me and kiss me. Unlike a lot of guys that I know I really enjoyed kissing, so I have spent a lot of time kissing so many girls.

So, I started to kiss Cally and was loving it as I always do.

Cally has the nicest and softest lips and was by far the best kisser I ever had the pleasure to kiss. I could just lay there and hug and kiss Cally for hours and be happy.

I slip my cock in Cally hot wet pussy and in under two minutes filled her with my loving cum. I could tell that Cally was having a nice time, although I thought that maybe she liked the kissing better then the sex, but I was not sure.

As my cock deflated, I laid my head down on Cally shoulder and kissed her left breast a little while I rubbed Cally's right breast with my hand. Cally seemed to really enjoy that for a few minutes, then I just laid there and hugged her for about 10 minutes until I could get another erection.

I moved back on top of Cally and started kissing her again and Cally seemed extra hungry for me this time. My cock got like iron after just a few kisses and I reentered Cally and fucked her real slow and real lovingly.

Cally was moaning up a storm this time and was moving her hips in conjunction with mine and whispered to me that she loves to feel my inside her like this. I was able to fuck Cally this time for about 5 minutes before I came and filled Cally's nice pussy with my second load of cum.

We took a shower together and watched some TV and fell asleep in one another's arms again, for maybe the last time.

At breakfast, I did not eat much as I was very nervous. I asked Cally to drive me to the Reform Farm that morning for several reasons. First, I did not think I was in any condition to drive as I was really nervous and very scared and even feeling sick. As a result, I needed Cally's company and her strength to get me though that part of my day.

The second reason is that she would know where the Reform Farm was so that she could come and visit with me, if she wanted to. I was sure hoping she wanted too.

The last reason that I told Cally was that she could bring my car home as I will not be needed a car for the next four years. Accordingly, Cally, here is the title to my car as I have signed it over to your mother, as Molly only has that broken down old car.

Mort, you are giving my mother a $90,000.00 Jaguar? Yea, Cally, I am.

Cally started to cry and she just cried and cried and cried some more. A few minutes went by before Cally could speak and told me that she cannot believe me as after what Ally did, that I am being so good to her and her family.

Again, I had to sit there for a few more minutes while

Cally cried. Then I just took her by the hand and walked her out to the car.

INTRODUCTION TO THE REFORM FARM:

As Cally was driving me to the Reform Farm I was really depressed and nervous and upset as I thought I would be. I think that I was more upset about not see Cally any more, then I started to cry as not seeing Cally anymore was breaking my heart.

Cally looked over at me, but did not say anything. Cally just took my hand in hers and that calmed me down some. We drove up route 75 for about 60 miles and then took a small road about 10 miles west of the interstate and then we saw the sign for the Reform Farm.

Cally got out of the car and came around to my side and opened the door and told me to get out that she needed a kiss. That made me smile and I dragged myself out of the car.

Cally stepped up to me and pushed me up against the car and kissed me and kissed me like she meant to kiss me, like she really cared about me. We just stood there for a few minutes making out in the parking lot and then Cally spoke to me.

MORT, tell me you will be brave for ME! Cally made me smile and I even got a tear in my right eye and I looked at her and told her that I would do my best for "YOU", Cally.

Cally looked into my eyes and just said, good Mort, see that you do. Leaving all me stuff in the car, Cally took my hand and walked me up to the front door like she was walking a child into the dentist office.

The house was a very large and very nice log home made from very nice large logs. In the front of the house was a very large covered wood deck. As Cally and I walked up the steps to the front door, Cally paused and then told me to go and stand in that corner over there.

For some reason, I just obeyed Cally and walked over and stood in the corner, like I was little kid. Cally knocked on the front door. A woman answered the door and Cally introduced herself and told the lady that she was delivering Morton as scheduled, but that she wished to see the Boss first.

The lady invited Cally inside and the door closed. I would guess that I stood in that corner for over a half hour before that lady came out to get me and took me inside.

I had no idea as to what Cally and whoever was inside spoke about or why it took so long. I was really surprised that they spoke at all as what did Cally have to do with my prison time there on that farm I wondered?

Nevertheless, I figured that Cally could do no harm and could only help, so it was all good as far as I was concerned. After All, at that point in time, Cally seemed to be in control of my life and has been doing a pretty good job of navigating me thru all of my problems.

The women who came to get me was a nice looking older lady, maybe 45 years old. Yes, that is old to me, as I was about to turn only 20 . Her name was Anne and she had a very nice figure and wore a white long sleeve blouse with ruffles in the front together with a tight black skirt about half way up from her knees.

Anne also wore about 4 inch high heels and had a great pair of bare legs and looked like she still had a nice ass for a women that age and she medium size tits, that gave her a nice figure. Anne had very nice past the shoulder length brown hair and a nice smile. Over all, she looked really well kept for a lady of her age.

The lady took me to an office where a man was sitting behind a desk and Cally was sitting in a chair in front of the desk. The man told me to stand next to Cally and Cally took my hand.

The man behind the desk was about 50 years old, a clean cut looking black haired man. The man told me the following:

Mort, first I would like to tell you that I have had the most wonderful discussion with your friend Cally. You are a lucky boy to have such a friend, son. I was too scared to say anything so I just squeezed Cally hand and the man noticed that and smiled a little.

Mort, Cally tells me that even though you signed all the admission papers to come here that you have not read them and have just came here because Cally told you to. Yes, Sir.

Mort, I want you to understand a few things that will

help you with your stay here. I want you to always remember that we get paid very well for teaching you to behave. We will do almost anything to teach you to behave, except injure you in any way.

That is not to say that we will not use corporal punishment here as we will. That corporal punishment part surprised me as I did not think they used such methods in prisons anymore, even though I did remember reading something about that when I signed the papers. However, I thought I was too upset at the time to really notice what anything said and I just signed because Cally told me to.

I guessed that maybe this place was different and that's why they could use such measures. I was not happy to hear that I may be punished with the use of corporal punishment. However, I did think it was alright for me to punish the girls that way, so should it not be alright for me to be punished that way?

The Boss continued, Mort, in fact, as you apparently believed yourself that corporal punishment was a quick and easy way to teach others obedience, you should appreciate our methods.

Additionally, Mort, as I understand that you expected complete obedience from Ally and Sabrina and Cally. So too now, Mort, you should now appreciate that is all we expect from you on this farm, that is complete and prompt and polite obedience, nothing more and nothing less.

Mort, you may wish to keep in mind that just as you enjoyed punishing Sabrina and Ally, and Cally, that we too also enjoy our jobs here and will enjoy punishing you just the same. So, Mort, you have been warned and you know what to expect if you are disobedient. So now it's all up to you.

Mort, also remember, the state pays us for converting bad boys into good boys and the better job we do the more bad boys they send us and the more money we make. So, as you can imagine, our incentive it great not to have any failures.

During our first five years in this business, Mort, we have not failed to convince even one bad boy to become a good boy and we do not expect you to become our first failure, is that understood Mort? Yea, ok, I said.

Additionally, Mort, your friend Cally here tells me that you will be the most obedient boy that we ever had here on the farm before you leave us and that she will see to it. I had no clue as to why Cally had anything to do with this, but I surely was not going to say anything.

If Cally made him some promise that I would become a good obedient boy and that was going to help me somehow, it was fine with me. Cally seemed to know what's best for me at that point in my life, even better than me, I was learning.

At the same time I gave the man that flip answer, I was somewhat scared of him, as I was also scared of this place as I did not really know what to expect. As far as that corporal punishment part, I have been spanked by my dad, but that's all. I had no interest in finding out how much a strap or cane may hurt, so I figured being obedient should not be too hard.

Alright Mort we are not off to a good start here. Your answer to everybody, other than other bad boys, around here is very simple, yes Sir, Yes Miss, got it Mort. Yea ok, then I caught myself and said, yes Sir. The man just smiled at me and said, remember the part about us loving our work around here Mort as it will serve you well. Yea, Yea I thought, but kept my mouth shut.

Alright Mort, lets cover some of the rules, OH YEA, the man said, there is only one rule. You, Mort, you will very simply say yes sir or yes Miss and then obey each and every order anybody gives you and you will do so each and every time and there are no excuses and no exceptions and you will never be forgiven for any breach of this obedience rule. Got it Mort?

I was feeling a bit more uneasy with this guy, so I was a bit more polite with his, yes Sir. Mort, just so there are no misunderstandings, doing anything other then what you are told to do is the same as disobedience. so, if you think that maybe you should be doing something that you were not specifically told to do, ASK! FIRST! MORT!

If this guy was trying to scare me, it was working as I was getting even more nervous by the minute. Alright the man said, now let me tell you the stages of becoming a good boy so you will know what to look for during your stay with us.

During the first step, you will be yourself Mort, the same you, with the same attitude, that got you sent here. You will rebel and my guess is that you in particular will rebel more often than most. When you rebel, you will be punished. As I noted earlier, Mort, we love to punish bad boys around here so we hope you rebel often so we can punish you a lot.

The second step, will be obedience. You will learn to obey because you will find out that you will always find obedience that easier path, always, no matter what. The only choice you will have is to decide is if you want to get punished before you obey.

In other words, if someone tells you to do something and you do not immediately say yes sir or yes Miss and do it, or if you refuse to do it, then we will punish you and then you will do it anyway. Mort, I think that is the same rule that you had in your house, so you should understand the concept very well.

Then Mort, over time you will learn it is better to obey promptly the first time, so you can skip the punishment as punishments around here are only fun for us, not you. Again Mort, that theory should sound familiar to you as it was the same theory you had with Sabrina and Ally and Cally. After you had your fun, they learned to obey you. The same will be true here, only for you to learn.

The third step, will be when you actually enjoy pleasing those that give you orders and actually enjoy doing the work for them. That does not mean that you will always enjoy the work, only that you will enjoy doing it as is makes your Boss happy. When you get to that point in your life, then you will be ready to leave here.

Now that we are friends, the man said, my name is BOSS! to you. Miss Anne, the lady that let you in the front door is Miss to you. Everyone else is Sir to you, got it Mort? Yes Boss and I was very quiet and polite in my response.

I started to ask a question but as the Boss saw me open my mouth, he interrupted my thoughts by telling me, NO! Mort! There are no questions from you, just obedience, got it? Yes Boss.

Alright then, you can go now. Miss Anne is waiting for you outside and will get you started. As I started to turn away to leave, the man said, Mort, do you remember what the rules are? Yes Boss, obedience, I said. Very good Mort, keep telling yourself that over and over and over again, it may help you, although I doubt it, now go on. Yes Boss, I replied.

Cally and I exited the office back into the living room and Miss Anne stood up and came over to me and told me to follow her and I said yes Miss and followed her out the front door. As we exited the front door on to a large front patio wood deck there were two men standing there.

They were both very large fellows, both about 6 foot 4 inches tall and very muscular. One was white and the other one was a black guy. They both had muscles on top of muscles and must have weighed about 225 pounds to 240 pounds compared to me at 5 foot 7 inches tall and 127 pounds.

Miss Anne told me to take off all my clothes. I was so surprise by Miss Anne's request that I just looked around wondering if I was suppose to get undressed right her on the porch in front of everyone else. I looked at Cally and Cally just looked at me like what am I waiting for?

So, as I took off all my clothes. Miss Anne told me to leave my socks and sneakers on. I remembered to say Yes Miss that time. Once I was naked Miss Anne told me to go to my car and bring in everything that I brought with me. Still standing there naked, I asked, I'm naked where are my new clothes?

Miss Anne did not respond to me, rather she just turned around and nodded to the two big guys. The two big guys did not say a word to me or Miss Anne, but they came over behind me and with one on each side of me they just picked me up by the my arms and took me right down the stars of the porch.

They carried me over to what looked like an old time wood hitching post for horses. It was about 3 feet high and had just one cross bar supported on the two ends by a wood post in the ground. The hitching post was about 25 yards from the front porch right in the middle of the yard.

The two giants put me naked, as naked could be, down and I was now figuring that maybe it would have gone easier for me if I had just obeyed Miss Anne when she told me to go get the stuff out of my car, even if I was naked. So, I would have been embarrassed, big deal, right?

Both men picked up leather cuffs that were hanging from the hitch post. They were leather wrist and ankle cuffs which were the same kind that I used on the girls at home. These two guys attached one to each of my wrists and one to each of my ankles.

Then one of them just pushed me over the cross bar and

I landed on the bar with only my waist balancing me on the cross bar. Before I had any time to think about what was happing, the two men attached my ankle cuffs to hooks in the ground and I could not move my legs at all. They came around to the front. I tried to get back up in a reflex move, but one of them pushed me in the back so I could not get up.

They then attached my two wrist cuffs to hooks in the ground in front of me but to the side of my head so my arms were stretched out ahead of me but about 3 feet apart, just like my feet were apart. My hips rested on the bar, my ass was sticking up in the air and I could not move even a inch in any direction.

The next thing I knew I heard an explosion and a tremendous pain in my butt. Again and again and again an explosion and yet more tremendous pain. One of the giants was beating my ass with a thick leather strap. I had never been punished with a strap before so this was all new to me and not in a good way.

That Giant must have hit me 10 times and I was struggling and breathing hard, and trying to get away with all the strength I had. But, I could not move at all, cuffed to the ground the way I was.

The giant kept beating me with that strap and by the time he hit me 15 times or so I burst into tears and started crying like Ally cried when I would strap her. I could not believe it, I was 19 years old and I was crying like a little girl.

But the pain was unbearable and the sound of the CRACK! CRACK! CRACK! CRACK! CRACK! was really very loud. The licks just kept on coming followed by more and more and more pain. I could not believe how much the strap was hurting me.

The guy stopped strapping me as I laid there crying very heavy, like I had never cried before in my life. I thought my pain was going to stop, but he just handed the strap over to the other giant and the other giant started to strap my ass from the other side and all I could hear was CRACK! CRACK! CRACK! CRACK! CRACK! And all I could do was absorb the pain while I cried and cried and cried and struggled in vain to move even an inch in any direction.

The second giant gave me about another CRACK! CRACK! CRACK! CRACK! CRACK! 20 More CRACKS! and then he stopped. It was quiet at that point as far as the strap was concerned, but I was still crying my head off just like a little girl with snot running out of my nose and dripping all over the ground competing to make a bigger puddle then my tears. MAN! My ass just hurt and hurt and was pounding in pain.

After a few minutes, when I was calming down and my crying was almost finished I thought that those guys left and I was all alone as it was real quiet. Being bound in this position was not very comfortable, but that was nothing compared to the pain in my ass cheeks.

I looked over to the porch and thru my tears saw Cally and the Boss sitting on rocking chairs enjoying an ice tea. I felt so strange having Cally sit there and watch me get punished that way.

I felt so extra embarrassed and humiliated and shamed

to be strapped like that in front of Cally. As much as I wanted Cally to stay longer, I now wished she would leave to take away my shame and humiliation of crying like a little girl in front of her.

So, I was left there all tied up in the front yard where anybody who came by would be able to see me. Just in case that happened, I kept my head down and just looked at the ground so that I would not be able to see anyone, see me.

But, I knew Cally was still there chatting with the Boss watching me and my bare ass sticking up in the air with all those welts from the strapping.

I started to wonder if Cally enjoy watching me get punished like she enjoyed watching me punish Sabrina and Ally. I wondered if Cally was enjoying watching me cry, like she enjoyed watching Sabrina and Ally cry. I was wondering if Cally enjoyed looking at my ass with all those new bright red welts like she enjoyed looking at Sabrina's and Ally's.

About 15 minutes later the Boss came over to me and asked, are you ready to obey now. As I sniffled thru my clogged nose I said, yes Boss.

The Boss unhooked me and helped me to my feet. Then he told me to go to the car and get all my stuff and put it all on the porch. Yes Boss, I sniffled and dragged my well strapped and sore ass to the car. I knew Cally was watching the whole thing and I was so humiliated for her to see me like this. So, full of shame.

That was the first time I saw the Boss standing up and

he was also a very big guy as well. He was not as well muscled as the other two, but he was about 6'1" and well over 220 pounds or so, also all muscle.

It took me three trips to the car to bring everything to the porch. I really felt out of place as I was still naked and the other five people were all fully clothed. Additionally, I had a fully strapped ass and a face full of dried tears and red eyes for all to see, even Cally.

The Boss looked at all my stuff and then told me that I could keep the TV, the computer, and the DVR, and everything else was to be put back in the car as I would not be needing them.

The Boss turned towards Cally and told her to give all that stuff away as I would never be needing any of it again. WHAT? I said, they are all the clothes I have with me and they are real expensive too!

Before I even had time to realize that the Boss was not happy with my outburst the two big guys picked me back up by my arms and took me back to the hitching post and reattached my wrists and ankles to the ground once again.

Without a word, CRACK, CRACK, CRACK, CRACK, CRACK, CRACK, CRACK, CRACK. I was not sure that this strapping hurt any more then the last time since my ass was already sore, but it sure hurt just as much.

CRACK, CRACK, CRACK, CRACK, CRACK, CRACK, CRACK, CRACK, I thought that the Boss was correct that they will enjoy punishing me as the one giant was strapping me about a hard as one could and if he thought that he was punishing me and teaching me a lesson and hurting me as much as he could then he was correct as this was just simply horrible, it hurt so much and I could not do anything about it.

CRACK, CRACK, CRACK, CRACK, CRACK, CRACK, CRACK, CRACK, CRACK, CRACK! All I could do was lay there over that wood rail and suffer and cry and cry and cry and cry some more. I guess this is what the Boss meant when he said that they all enjoy their jobs of punishing Bad Boys and I was being punished and punished like I never thought possible. CRACK, CRACK, CRACK, CRACK, CRACK, CRACK, CRACK, CRACK, CRACK!!!!! CRACK!!!!!!!!!

I thought that after about the first 30 additional licks that my ass got so swollen that it was not hurting so much anymore. Only where the tail of the strap would wrap around and hit the side of my ass was still hurting and still hurting a whole lot.

This second strapping of the morning finally came to an end after about 40 more hard licks of the big thick strap, my ass was just pounding in pain. The two guys walked away and left me there again to just hang over that wood cross bar and cry some more as the pain in my ass from that strapping was just too much for me to handle.

About 5 minutes later after I stopped crying for the second time that morning, Cally came over to me and bent down in front of me and told me to life my head. As I lifted my head and saw Cally's pretty face, and she saw my tear stained face, I felt all humiliated again, even more so as she was right there looking at me.

Mort, you have only been here for an hour and you have been disobedient twice. Maybe obedience was not as easy as you once thought? Nevertheless, Mort, you have already learned that they are not kidding about you being completely obedient, so you better be completely obedient or you are going to learn the hard way.

Mort, I am going to leave now. I have been told that you cannot have visitors for the first 30 days, so I will come back and visit you on August 1st. Meanwhile, Mort, obey them and be brave for me.

Cally? yes Mort? Thank you for everything Cally, you are the absolutely the finest of all of God creations. Cally, gave me a big smile and thank you Mort, thank you, I will see you again on August 1st.

Cally got up and walked away and said goodbye to the Boss on her way to the car. Apparently the two guys put all my stuff back in the car for Cally and she drove away and left me to my punishment. I was actually happy that Cally left as I was so extra humiliated with her there. However, I was disappointed that I would not get to see her for another 30 days.

The Boss came back in about 15 minutes and asked me if I was ready to be obedient yet. YES SIR! was all he heard. The Boss told the two giants that they could have me now and they unhooked me and helped me to my feet.

The two giants took me to show me my room. The rooms for the inmates which were outside the main house on the east side. The rooms were just a line of rooms like you would see with a motel. There were 15 rooms in total.

Miss Anne opened the door to show me the inside and as I walked in I was shocked. I don't know what I expected but all that was in the room was just a small bed, a sheet, a pillow case and pillow, and a blanket.

There was a toilet, a small sink, and a shelf over the sink, and nothing else, just bare cinder block walls. Oh, there was a small light on the ceiling and a thermostat on the wall. Last, there was one wall receptacle.

The two giants told me to go back to the porch and get my stuff and put them in my room and then the one giant pointed over to a barn and said, you see that barn over there, go over to the barn and you can get some lunch and then Pete will give you a job to do.

I also started to ask a question but shut my mouth and just said yes Sir. I took two trips to the porch to get my three items and put them in my room. Then I walked slowly over to the barn.

The barn was about 100 yards from where we were standing so it took a few minutes for me to get there, but during the entire walk I could feel more pain in my butt cheeks as I walked and made them move.

I was also concerned about my clothes, any clothes at this point as I was walking across some field completely naked with only a big bruised and hurting butt to cover any of my white skin.

I got to the barn and both the giants were there eating, there was one guy wearing a big white apron like a cook behind a counter, and 4 other guys dressed in just shorts and T shirts sitting their eating.

There was also one other guy, who was also naked, who was standing in a corner with his hands held up high over his head secured by wrist cuffs to a hook in the wall.

That guy had big red welts all over his ass from a strap just like me. I guessed that I was not the only disobedient one that day. As it turned out there was two of us that were naked that day, so I had some company. Not that it made me feel all that much better about my hurting ass and my own embarrassment about being naked.

But, for some strange reason I did notice that the guy standing in the corner had a real nice ass and I liked looking at it. I especially enjoyed it with all those bright red welts all over it. So, I guess I thought that it was not just female asses that I liked looking at after they were punished, it was male asses as well, interesting?

I had to put my back to the other guys as I faced the counter to get my lunch and I was totally humiliated standing there naked with a freshly strapped ass to show off to all these other guys. I was not homophobic at all but I was still embarrassed to no end to be naked in front of a bunch of guys who all had least some clothes on.

As I was standing there with my own strapped ass on display, about 6 or 7 other guys came in for lunch and although they did not say anything to me, I knew they were all checking me out and that did not help with my humiliating factor at all.

I got some fried chicken, some corn and some macaroni and cheese. I sat down at a table that was empty as I did not know any of these guys and considering the last hour of my life, I did not want any company. I felt more pain in my ass when I sat down, but at least the food was good.

I did notice that one of the other guys was not wearing a shirt and had some nasty looking bruises on his back left over from welts when he obviously got a strapping about a week or so ago. But, I did note that those strap marks were on his back and not on his ass and thought that it was a strange place to strap a guy, why not his ass?

While I sat there eating I could hear some of the other guys taking and saying that I was a big sissy. Apparently Pete or Rick, as I found out the names of the two giants, told everybody that I cried like a little girl when I was strapped. Apparently the other guys did not cry when they were strapped and therefore they consider me to be a sissy for crying.

Maybe they were right, I had no way of knowing, but it was humiliating nevertheless just knowing that everybody thought that way about me. Maybe next time I am punished I will try real hard not to cry, this time I just let nature take its course and I cried, I cried like I never cried in my whole life.

After lunch Pete told me to go with this other guy, John, yes Sir. As we left the barn that guy who was standing in the corner was still there and I got a better look at his ass and it was just covered all over from top to bottom and from side to side with nasty looking welts about 2 inches wide from the strap.

John and I spent the rest of the afternoon moving hay

bundles from a truck into the barn and then had to used pitch forks to spread some of the hay around. John worked at a leisurely pace so I just followed along. Later in the afternoon we even put some hay in a pickup truck and spread it out over an area in the field that had some cows.

I asked John about where to get shorts as I was still naked and he told me that he minds his own business and I should too. John said that if and when they want me to have shorts to wear that they will give them to me.

Otherwise, John said, just obey every order promptly and politely, or not only will your ass always look like that, but your back will too. Then John looked at me and told me that after a guy get punished he is usually kept naked for ten days. If he is good for ten days in a row then he gets his clothes back.

We finished our jobs with the hay by 5:15 according to the clock on the wall, so John laid down on a bale of hay and said he was going to take a nap before dinner which was at 6 pm. Is that alright to take a nap, I asked.

John said that as long as you finish what you were told to do for that day, that it was alright to rest, after all John added, we are in Florida and it is very hard to work all day in the heat without taking breaks and they know that. The important thing is to finish your work, don't ever even think about not finishing your work, not ever, John added!

John and I went back to the barn at 6 pm to get dinner, but Pete told me that I had to stand in the corner as I was punished that day and for the next three nights as well at dinner time. I was not happy about this news, but standing in the corner was better than getting another beating. My face turned beat red from being embarrassed by the news however, but all Pete heard was, yes Sir.

Pete took me over the corner and put the wrist cuffs back on both of my wrists and then lifted them up over my head and hooked them to a rope that was hanging down from the ceiling rafter. Pete then adjusted the ropes length so that my hands were held just above my head against the wall. My back was facing all the guys having dinner.

I had to stand in the corner until all the other guys had their dinner and left the barn, so it was about 30 to 40 minutes all together. My shoulders were getting tired of being up over my head for so long and my legs were getting tired of just standing there, but what was I to do except try to stay out of trouble going forward.

The next afternoon at lunch that same guy was back standing in the corner. Apparently he had three lunches of corner time, so he had one more after that day. I still had two more days of corner time at dinner time and was not looking forward to that, but as I said, what could I do?

Those thoughts started me thinking about how Sabrina and Ally must have felt when I made them stand in the corner. Especially when they had to hold her dresses up to show off the spanked or canned or strapped asses.

Even more so, on one the unlucky occasions that

someone came to front door and saw them standing in the corner. That must have been very humiliating for them. I sure thought I was alright to humiliate them like that, but, now that it is me being humiliated, I did not like it so much.

Other than having to stand in the corner for the next tow dinner times and still being naked all the time, my first ten days went by without further incident. I showed up at the barn every morning by 8 am as we were suppose to and I did whatever work was assigned to be by Rick or Pete that day. Mostly I worked with John and we cleaned the barn each morning of all the horse crap and feed the horses and made sure they had water.

We would use the pickup truck to move hay around to different areas where there were horses in the fields and cows in different places. We feed the donkeys and the goats and the pigs and cleaned up there areas. We also feed the Alpacas. I really liked the Alpacas as they were neat looking and friendly.

By the way, the barn with all the hay and the animals was a different barn then the barn that we all ate in. The barn we ate in was just for the guys and had showers and the kitchen and all the picnic tables. There was also a few nasty looking straps hanging from the walls as well as a few whips and a bunch of wrist and ankle cuffs.

When my first ten days were over I did not get any shorts to wear and was wondering why, but was afraid to ask, so I kept my mouth shut. I was use to being naked at this point, but I still did not like it especially as the other guys would make comments about how small my penis was and how nice my ass looked with all those welts.

Even though the welts were fading, it was obvious that I was given a good hard strapping. The next morning I asked John about why I was not getting any shorts and he told me that he understood that I was actually punished twice that first day. I told him that was true and he told me that's why I was not getting a shorts, as I had to wait 20 days, ten days for each punishment.

I was not happy about that, but then I could do nothing about it and as I said I was getting use to being naked. The other guys were getting use to me as well as I did not hear the comments about me being a sissy or having a small penis as time went by.

My next ten days move along without anything worth mentioning as it was becoming more of the same every day. I continued to work with John feeding and cleaning up after the animals. The other guys did other jobs like cleaning the Boss car, making the food and cleaning up the guys barn. Some of them cut the grass on large open fields and picked oranges and other fruit. Some of them chopped logs into fire wood.

Well, actually they used chain saws to cut the logs up and used a splitter to make the fire wood. Apparently the fire wood business was one of the ways the farm made money. Apparently, being in Florida and not needing fire wood very often the farm did not have any competition and with the free labor had no problem selling the fire wood for less than anyone else could.

Most of the fruit and vegetables that were grown in the

farm went to feed us guys along with the Boss and Miss Anne. I guessed that would keep their food bill down and again with free labor did not cost much to produce. The Alpaca's fur was sold off for good money from what I heard and the chickens and pigs, etc, well you can guess why they raised them.

On my 21st day I was finally eligible to get clothes to wear. Rick told me to see the Boss after lunch. After lunch I walked down to the house and was hopeful of getting some clothes to wear. I have been naked now for 20 days and I was sort of use to it, but I would prefer clothes.

I knocked on the front door and Miss Anne let me in and took me to the Boss's office. The Boss told me to wait as he seemed very frustrated with his computer as it did not seem to be working.

Excuse me Sir? WHAT MORT? I am pretty handy with computers, may I take a look for you? The Boss looked at me and thought for a minute and said sure Mort, as the Boss seemed much more civil to me. I fixed it for him for him in about three minutes.

After that the Boss was a lot more friendly with me and we talked about how I had been getting along during my first 21 days? I told the Boss, with the exception of the first day, things have gone a lot smoother for me.

I told him that I never did manual labor before, but that I would get use to it. The Boss told me that unlike in a real prison, that everybody here is expected to get along and be nice to each other.

Mort, you will not need to worry about anyone sexually

abusing you or beating you up to asking for protection money, or any of the other bad things that happen in real prisons. Around here Mort, you get along or you get punished, so everyone gets along.

However, while we were chatting about some of the other kids on the Farm the Boss told me that everyone on this Farm belongs here except this one kid named LeMond Stillmen.

According to the Boss, LeMond was there on a drug charge but that he was not guilty. However, LeMond got three years here as he would not tell the police who really owned the drugs that were found in the trunk of his car.

So, I figured that LeMond was either protecting a family member or he was protecting someone because he is afraid that they will hurt his family or hurt him if he told the truth. Later that day I was thinking that maybe I could get Cally to look into LeMond's case and see if the Boss was correct.

The Boss gave me some clothes to wear that matched what the other guys Wore and I put the extra things in my room and went back to work.

As I got to the barn for lunch, Pete told me that Cally was coming at 2 pm and that I should go to the house at that time, however, I was allowed to take a shower in the barn first so I did not smell bad. I took my shower and put on a clean T shirt and clean shorts and underwear and walked over to the house.

As I walked down the driveway to the house I could see Cally sitting on the porch waiting for me and I was so extra excited. I had missed her so much, so much more than I ever thought that I would.

As I walked up the steps, Cally jumped up and gave me a big smile and even gave me a real nice long loving kiss. Cally stepped back and asked if I had been a good boy after that first day and I blushed a little and told her yes.

Good Mort, that is good news, so let's go inside and I will give you a nice blow job for being such a good boy, as Cally looked at me and licked her lips and UMMMMM!!!!

As soon as we entered the office Cally dropped right to her knees and pulled my shorts and underwear down and found herself a erect cock. Cally looked up at me and smiled and told me that she missed my cock. As you could imagine, my cock was leaking pre cum already as it had been hard as a rock since Cally gave me that long sweet kiss on the porch.

Cally moved her mouth towards my cock and smiled at me and licked her lips and took my cock in her mouth and lubricated it very quickly with her mouth and tongue.

Cally took my entire cock in her mouth and started to face fuck my cock and within two minutes or so I was rewarding Cally's hungry mouth with a mouthful of my cum. Just as my cock expanded to cum, Cally seemed to get all excited and moaned and move her head not just up and down but all around as well, as she sucked my cum out of me. Damn, that Cally was a great cock sucker, I thought.

However, Cally was not finished with me as she would not let my cock out of her mouth as she just kept sucking on it gently and actually stopped it from getting soft with her actions.

Cally kept me cock almost full size by continuing to work it over with her lovely lips and very talented mouth and tongue. After a few minutes Cally let my cock slid out of her mouth as she sucked hard on it to get every last drop of cum off it.

Cally pushed my shorts back up into place and told me to sit down. We sat on the couch together and Cally told me to tell her what I have been doing for the past 31 days.

Cally, if you don't mind, before I tell you about me, how

is Toni doing. OH! Mort. Toni, is doing well, considering what she has been though. But Mort, it is so sad.

First, Mort, your idea of having Toni come and live with me was a great idea as I have enjoyed the personal company now that you are not there.

Additionally, it has been better for Toni, as again you were correct, if she stayed home her care would not have been as good. I have the nurse visit her every other day whereas at home, she only was seeing someone every week or longer.

However, you know Mort, from the Chemo, her hair fell out, she lost weight and looks unhealthy. However, now that all that has ended, the doctor believes that she will regain her strength and hair and healthy look in over the next few months.

OH, another thing Mort, Toni got her notice that she was accepted into my university and she could not have been happier. Toni, could not believe her luck when she found out that some charity paid for her tuition as well. She still has no idea that you paid for saving her life and saving her family's home and paid for her tuition as well.

Mort, I know it is your principle that you don't let people know where the charity came from so that they don't feel that they owe you anything, but sooner or later Toni will find out that she had no grant and then what do I tell her.

Cally for now, nothing. Toni will not find out for a

year until next year's tuition is due, We will think of something by then.

Mort, I have one more thing here to add to this conversation as well. What else did you do to get Ally and Toni accepted? I know it was not just dumb luck that there was two empty spots and you were lucky enough to be there on the right day to pay for them? I just looked at Cally and asked, what else could have I possibly done?

Cally looked at me like she did not believe me, but did not know what to say. Alright Mort, tell me about your last 31 days. Well, Cally, after you left that first day I was kept naked for the next 20 days. Apparently around here, when you are punished, you are kept naked for 10 days, so I was punished twice, thus the 20 days.

How did you feel about being naked in front of all these guys, Mort? Cally, The guys around here are not allowed to tease you directly, but they do talk among themselves and I can hear them. So, they teased me indirectly about me having a small penis.

That's alright Mort, you know that's one of the reasons I really like you penis, it fits in my mouth so well. It's big enough to fill me mouth completely, but not big enough so it's too much for me to handle, so it's perfect for us, Mort. So, Mort, don't let that bother you, what else Mort?

Cally, then they teased me about being a sissy as I cried when I was punished. Apparently those guys can take a beating like that and just yell and grunt, but not cry. So, apparently I am the exception around here, so they call me sissy behind my back.

Mort, do you remember how you use to enjoy standing in front of us after you punished one of us and how much you enjoyed watching us cry? Sure, Cally. Well, Mort, as you know I am always honest with you, even when I know you will not like the message. I know Cally, believe me, I know.

Well, Mort, when I sat on the porch that day and watched Pete and Rick give you that terrible strapping, I have to tell you Mort, I love watching you cry. Mort, I loved listening to you cry. And Mort, when I went down on my knee in front of you before I left and saw you crying face I thought I was going to have an orgasm right there. I had to drive home with soaking wet panties and I have masturbated several times since then as I thought about watching you cry that day.

So, Mort, don't worry your pretty head about what they think. Instead think about what I think and maybe that will help you ignore them. Cally, does that mean you also enjoyed watching me get punished like I use to enjoy punishing Sabrina and Ally.

Cally, smiled at me. Mort, yes. Mort, I am sorry in a way as I felt bad for you, but yes I did enjoy it a lot and found it to be very exciting. Sorry Mort.

Cally, don't be sorry. It is not like you feel that way on purpose, or that you would have someone beat me just for you own fun. You just enjoyed watching a disobedient boy get a licking that he earned himself, so it's fine Cally, don't be sorry.

Cally you know that when you earned a punishment, that I loved punishing you, and I enjoyed your pain, and I enjoyed watching you cry. So, this is no different, just reversed.

Cally, just as you are trying to tell me not to worry about the crying as you enjoy that, I think I will be able to take my punishments better now that I know that you are enjoying them as for some reason, that makes it better for me, even if just a little bit better.

I guess Cally, what I am really thinking is that I would not be as embarrassed getting punished in front of you in the future now that I understand that you feel the same way about seeing me get punished as I did about punishing you or Sabrina or Ally.

Alight Mort, I am glad we had this conversation, now let's chat about the rest of you month. Cally, the other thing that happens around here after you are punished is that you need to stand in the corner, naked of course, during breakfast, lunch, or dinner in front of all the other guys as a message to them to behave and also to humiliate yourself. So, I had to stand in the corner, in front of all the guys, with my strapped ass on display for three dinners and that was no fun.

As far as the rest of the time, it is pretty much the same every day. All I can tell you Cally was that I did the same thing every day, which was spreading the hay and feeding all the animals and cleaned up after all the animals. I told Cally it was not real hard and that I did like the animals.

Cally asked me if anybody bothered me and I asked if

she meant did someone beat me up or threaten me or tried to have sex with me. Cally shook her head, yes. No, Cally, everyone is actually very nice, as long as you are obedient, you seem fine. I told Cally that the Boss told me that nothing like that stuff goes on around here and Cally was happy to hear it.

However, Cally, I do have two things that I would like you to look into. I told Cally about the story that the Boss told me about LeMond and how he is the only innocent one here on the farm.

So, Cally, what I would like you to do is hire that lawyer that we used and have him get a private detective to snoop around and see if he can determine who actually owed the drugs.

After that, tell them to figure out how to arrest that person and offer him a deal to take responsibility for LeMond arrest so we can get LeMond out of here without looking like LeMond told on them, which he did not.

Mort, you do realize that if the Boss finds out about this that he will punish you for doing something without his permission. Yes, Cally, I know, but what should I do? Nothing and let an innocent kid spend three years of his life here and then have a criminal record that he does not deserve for the rest of his life? Cally, I met the kid and he is a decent kid with a good attitude, even in here.

So, Cally, yes, I am willing to take my chances with the Boss to get an innocent kid out of here. Cally, LeMond does not belong here and it is just not fair. Alright Mort, I will do as you asked and let's see what happens.

Cally, the second thing is I would like you to have the detective look into all four of the people here. The Boss, Miss Anne, Rick and Pete. I would like to know as much about them as I can.

Sure, Mort, but why. No reason, Cally. My father taught me that he always had everyone he did business with investigated just to see what was out there about them. My dad would tell me that you never know what would turn up and the more you know about them the better off you are.

Alright, Mort, if you want me to, but you know the Boss will not be happy if he finds out you checked him out. Yes, Cally, I know, so tell the detective to be extra careful. Ok, Mort, I will handle it.

Alright Mort, I have a lot to show you and I need for you to sign some forms for me.

As Cally showed me a lot of pictures she told me that she had looked at five lots for the new house. Cally showed me five different lots that she looked at with my sister. Cally had plot plans, aerial photos, and tax information and many pictures to view.

After Cally showed me all five lots I picked out the one which I like much better than all the rest, but I did not say anything until Cally told me what my sister thought.

Cally gave me some additional information as to what

my sister thought and then Cally surprised me yet again when she told me that she liked the same one I liked.

Cally then looked right at me and said, in her loving yet strict tone that she showed me on a few occasions, Mort, I want to buy this one for me!

I guess, lucky for me, that was the one I liked too and also the one my sister liked the best. I was still stunned by Cally's "order" to me, but none the less I just said, Sure Cally, if that is the one you want.

I was still confused as to why I was buying the house for Cally and her family. Sure they could live there for the four years I was to stay on this farm. But, then they would be out of there and it would be my house and my sister's house, not their house? I found no reason to say anything to Cally as she seemed so happy and I was happy she was happy.

Now that that was settled, Cally was suppose to bring invoices for me to approve to be paid by the guardian at the bank who was in charge of all of my money and investments while I was at this prison farm for the next four years.

Cally, again, did as she wanted and not as I expected. Cally only brought copies of the invoices and already had the checks cut and gave me a form to sign as well.

Cally told me that she approved all of the invoices and all I had to do was sign the checks. I reviewed everything and found no fault with anything Cally did and signed all of the checks.

Then Cally told me that I just needed to sign the last form and we were almost finished. I looked at the last form and it took the rights of handling all of my money and investments from the bank and gave those rights to Cally.

I looked at Cally and before I could say anything, Cally said, MORT! I promise that I will not disappoint you, just as you have promised me you will be brave in accepting your punishment for me. Cally, handed me the pen and just looked at me. I could not say no to Cally and signed the forms.

Thank you, Mort, Cally said, your trust in me means more to me then you will ever know. Cally added, however, it will be much more convenient while paying all the bills as the new house is being built if I don't have to keep going to the bank all the time.

Alright Mort, let me show you the house plans now that we have decide on a lot. Cally showed me three different sets of plans by three different architects.

I looked at the first one and thought that it was alright, but it did not thrill me. The second one, I did not care for at all, not even a little. It looked real nice on the outside and the patio area was the best of the three, but I did not like how the interior was laid out at all.

I liked the third one, the best and I thought, we could combine the third house and the patio area of the second house and it would be perfect.

Alright Cally, which one did my sister like? Cally told

me that my sister picked out the same one I did. Alright then Cally I guess we have a choice.

No MORT! What Cally? What do you mean no? Well first of all Mort, you know when I say no I mean no! But, anyway, I decided that you were getting the second one. I was just speechless, I hated the second one and who was Cally to decide for me and my sister anyway? And what was with the bossy attitude I thought, it's my money and will be my house.

Mort, Cally said, tell me why you did not like the second house. Well Cally, it had the nicest patio area that I have ever seen and it looked the best from the outside. But, it was broken up too much on the inside more like pods and not one big house.

For the readers benefit, I will describe the house to you before I go on telling you about the conversation that followed with Cally as you will appreciate the rest of this part knowing the outlay of the house.

The first floor had two four car garage sets, four garages on each side of the middle of the home. However, the garage door were designed so they looked like they were part of the house and not garage doors. In the front middle of the house in between the 8 garage doors was a large stairway to the main floor, which was the second floor.

So when you looked at the front of the house as you came in the driveway you would see only the large stairway and entry area with four garage doors on each side. The purpose of this was that nothing that could be impacted by water could be on the first floor due to flooding concerns as the river over flows during storms every so many years.

However, behind the stairway on the first floor between the two garage areas, there was a very large lounge area with a stone floor and some of the pool. The pool was designed so that it was 75 feet long heading away from the house towards the river and was 20 feet wide. The beginning of the pool was under the house so that no matter the outside weather one could go swimming or sit out on the patio under the a roofed area of the home.

The rest of the pool extended outside of the first floor with a patio on both sides. However, the second 25 feet of the pool and patio was inside a screen enclosure. That way one could get some filtered sun and could be bug free while enjoying this part of the pool and or patio.

The last 25 feet of the patio and pool was out in the sun free of the screen enclosure. That way someone could enjoy the pool and patio in full sunlight, or moon light for that matter. Additionally, they could sit on the far part of the patio deck next to the river.

Considering how the rest of the house is designed the three patio and pool effect had other uses as you will see later. Last, there were two hot tubs installed under the screen part of the patio, as well as a nice outdoor grill set, including a refrigerator.

There was also a lot of storage areas along the garages and two bathrooms with full showers one for the ladies and one for the men for when someone has company and goes swimming or sunning or even out on a boat in the river, etc.

Last, the first floor had other rooms, one for a gym and a few other rooms that were water proofed that would be used for other purposes.

The second floor in the middle as you come in the front entrance, after you go up the stairs, there is a huge living room, with two circular staircases going to the second floor on each side of the living room.

Then as you pass thru the living room there is a back indoor patio. Then by going out the sliding glass wall in the back you are on an outside patio deck which was above the pool area.

One the right side of the living room was the kitchen with an indoor and outdoor eat in dining area. On the left side of the living room was large formal dining room and two offices.

There were two elevators, one on each side of the living room. One was convent for the left side of the house and the other for the right side of the house. You did not need to use the elevator however, as there were steps to all three floors as well from the garage.

Going further to the right of the living room behind the kitchen there was an apartment until itself. The complete apartment was about 3000 square feet and had 5 bedrooms, five and a half baths, its own smaller kitchen, its own office and its own indoor and outdoor patio area.

Above this second floor apartment was another apartment, the same 3000 square feet in size with the same layout. Both apartments had entrances from the main living room with the stairs or the elevator and additionally from the first floor garage so you really did not need to go into the main part of the house and could come and go thru the garage without seeing anyone else in the house. That was, as long as you don't need the elevator.

You could also use your own kitchen and the indoor and outdoor patios which were also private with walls in between so you could not see from one patio to the other. You could sunbath naked on you patio and no one could see you from another patio area.

On the other side of the living room, on the main floor, behind the offices and dining room, you would find two more individual apartments of 2000 square feet each. Both are set up just the first two only a little smaller, but had the same features and privacy provisions. Each had three bedrooms, three and a half baths, and an office.

Above those two apartments on the third floor were two more identical apartments. So there were four 2000 square foot pods and two 3000 square foot pods. That was my point as it was not all one house so to speak, as one would think, it was broken up into parts and every part had it own kitchen, how weird?

So, the bottom line here is that the house was set up sort of like an expensive apartment building, whereas there were 6 individual apartments which were self contained and private, including private entrances. Then there was the large common areas which anyone could use, including the pool areas.

The entire back of the house was all glass and the rooms were designed to provide that largest view of the river from the master bedrooms, and the living rooms.

I told Cally that I did not see the name of the architect on the bottom of the cover page for the second one, who was it? YES DAMN IT, CALLY SUPRISED ME AGAIN! Cally told me that she designed the house herself with a little input from my sister.

DAMN, DAMN, DAMN, what am I going to do with this Cally, she is just incredible. Cally deigned a very interesting house. But both my sister and I did not like it. Still, I respected the effort.

All right, now back to the conversation I had with Cally about her design. I tried not to be annoyed with Cally's attitude but she was basically telling me and my sister that we had to accept a house that cost 3 million dollars that we did not like.

Cally looked at me and said, Mort, just listen to me and I will tell you why you like this house the best. I just laughed a little and smiled at Cally and told her fine, Cally, go ahead. I thought that may be entertaining.

Cally told me that she designed the house that way as it accommodates the "not related" strange type of family that we have.

Yes, Cally, I know, because we are not really a family and this way we get separate areas but not separate housing. I continued to annoy Cally by still talking, but I continued, Cally, what happens when my four years are up and you are out of college, what then, sort of a funny house then don't you think Cally?

Cally, looked at me and said Mort, I want you to be quite until I am finished explaining and then you can speak. That sounded like an order and not a request, but I went along with Cally anyway, as I always do anymore.

Cally told me the following tale:

One, Mort, the name of the house is M&M Condo Assn, Inc.

(yes for Mort and Mindy)

Two, the house is set up to be a condominium association so that you will buy some of the units from the condominium association as follows. You will pay one and a half million dollars for one of the 3000 square foot units.

Three, you will pay, $750,000.00 each for two of the 2000 square foot units, or an additional $1.5 million dollars.

That would be you three millions dollar investment. Immediately upon closing on those units, the property value would then be a total of 6 million dollars, or double what you paid for the entire building as there are still three units that can be sold, one big one and two smaller ones.

Now, Mort, you are correct, this fits our current living

situation as we are not a real family, but we are people living in the same place, so it gives us unity and privacy all at the same time.

Now, Mort, when your four years is up, you can move into one of the pods or you can sell some or all of the units and move where ever you want with an extra 3 million dollars in your pocket.

So now Mort, what do you think NOW? I was stunned, just stunned, Cally was brilliant just brilliant, what an idea!!!!!!!!! What did my sister say Cally, I asked, after you explained it to her? She agreed with me. Cally, and you designed this yourself, yes Mort, I did.

I smiled and laughed and told Cally that she never stops surprising me and pleasing me at the same time. Very nice job, even a better job than all those "A"s you got last year in college.

I asked Cally how long it will take them to get started on the house after I sign the papers and DAMN! DAMN! DAMN! That Cally! Cally told me that they started two weeks ago. I started to laugh and smile and asked Cally so you have already made all the decisions and you were just letting me think that I had something to say about anything?

Cally, looked me in the eyes with that stern look she seems to be developing and said, that's correct, Mort.

I just laughed again and said, well Cally I guess over the past two months so you have taken over my life for me. Cally smiled and told me that was not true, not even close. Mort, I took over your life over a year ago, you just did not notice until now. Mort, you need a strong women to guide you and I have volunteered.

However, Cally added, Mort, tell me one time in your life I did anything that you have objected too. Well, she got me there, all I could say is that she was 100% correct and that was surly alright with me. Good Cally said, not waiting for an answer, I am happy to hear that, Mort.

Mort, I guess I need to be leaving. The Boss told me that I could have two hours to visit you and we are over that time already and he has not complained, so we should not take advantage.

The Boss told me that I may be able to have more time in the future, but it would depend on your behavior. However, before I go, I am still hungry and am going to treat myself to you cock once more.

Cally told me to take off my shorts and to sit in the chair. I did so and Cally got back on her knees in front of me. Cally gulped my stiff cock into her mouth like a vacuum cleaner.

Cally played with my balls with one hand and played with my cock with her mouth until I was hard again in under a minute. Then Cally would take my cock all the way into her mouth and throat and just hold it there for 30 seconds or so and let it out.

As Cally would look up to me and lick her lips and smile largely, she would take my cock all the way back in and just hold it there for up to a minute.

Cally kept doing this for about 5 minutes or so. It did feel good and I did like watching Cally's face up against my belly as she had my entire cock in her mouth. Every time Cally would take my cock back in her mouth she would be able to keep it deep within her mouth and throat for a longer period of time.

Cally started to bob up and down again and this time was taking me cock all the way in on every bob of her head and was face fucking my cock better than ever. DAMN! If Cally did not have me cuming again. WOW! What a cock sucking Cally gave me, she was terrific.

Cally kept sucking my cock gently as it deflated and as she usually does, sucks on it hard as she releases from her mouth so she can suck off any remaining cum. Cally, looked up at me again and gave me a big smile and licked her lips again and UUUMMMM!!!!

Cally got up and I got up and pulled my shorts back up. Mort, before I go, I have one other confession to make about that strapping and your future punishments and I was not sure if I should say this or not? Tell, me Cally, you know you can tell me anything.

Well, Mort, as I told you, I really enjoyed watching that strapping. However, I think it would have been even better for me if I was the one punishing you. In fact, Mort, I would prefer to be the one punishing you for all your Bad Boy behavior instead of these guys.

I smiled at Cally. Cally, since I am being punished for my Bad Boy behavior, I would prefer that as well. I would rather have you punish me then these guys also. I think that would be more correct then being punished by strangers.

After all, Cally, I was bad in our house with those who lived there and not with these strangers. So, Cally, I can understand how you feel and as embarrassing and humiliating it would be for me to be punished by you, it would be better than having Rick or Pete or the Boss punish me.

So, Mort, you are telling me that you would obey me and accept my decisions on you punishments? Cally, let's be honest with one another here. You are correct, you have been telling me what to do for over a year now and I have obeyed your every instruction, your every rule, your every order. Cally, to suggest that was not the case would just be pretending that reality was not reality. So, Cally, I guess the answer is yes, I would.

AND! Cally, you know what? That was the happiest and most fulfilling year of my life.

Cally started to get tears in her eyes and I did as well. So, Mort, you like my dominate personally? Cally, as I guess if this is confession day. I love your dominate personality Cally, I actually find it very exciting.

Cally started to cry a little harder so I just shut up and hugged her for a few minutes, enjoyed a few goodbye kisses and we left the office together.

As we walked out of the office, the Boss was there in the living room. As we walked over in front of the Boss, Cally looked at me and said, Mort, you can go back to work now, I am going to stay and speak with the Boss. I smiled at Cally and said good afternoon Boss, and left. I do not know what the Boss and Cally discussed or how long Cally stayed. I guess I will find out next time Cally visits.

FUCKING NIGGER:

The week after Cally visited, on the 8th of August, I had been at Reform Farm for 5 weeks. I was getting along pretty well with everyone and I was doing my job and I was avoiding getting punished.

I really enjoyed seeing Cally, MAN!, do I ever miss her. But at least I was feeling happy with myself that I was obeying Cally and staying out of trouble.

One morning after breakfast after most of the guys had left the barn to go back to work I was just chatting with two of the other guys when someone said something about How Rick seems to like to beat the white guys.

So, me, trying to fit in, said yea, I agree he is just a fucking nigger. Then there was silence in the barn and I felt someone behind me and I turned around and it was Rick.

Rick called Pete on his radio and Rick told me to wait for Pete outside the barn door. I knew I was in trouble and I did not need to make anything worse, so I got up and said yes Sir to Rick and went outside and waited for Pete.

Pete drove up on his horse and he dismounted with a rope in his one hand and wrist cuffs in the other. Pete walked over to me and said hold your hands out, yes sir. Pete put the wrist cuffs on my wrists.

Pete took the rope in his hand and I noticed the rope had a metal clip on the one end and Pete used the clip to clip the rope to my wrist cuffs which held my hands together out in front of me. Then Pete ripped off my shorts and shirt so I was naked once again.

Pete got back up on his horse and started the horse walking and I had no choice but to follow the about 50 feet behind the horse, as the horse pulled me along. We walked about a hundred yards when I noticed a lot of mud in front of the horse and the horse was headed right towards the big mud area which was about the size good sized swimming pool, maybe 20 feet by 40 feet. I could only assume that Pete was going to make me walk thru all that mud as he was walking me around for punishment for calling Rick a nigger.

As it turned out, I was wrong about the mud, Pete did not make me walk thru the mud. Instead Pete made the horse go much faster causing me to fall to the ground and Pete dragged me thru the mud and I got all muddy as you could imagine. I had mud all over me as Pete went even faster causing me to roll over and over in addition to being pulled forward very quickly.

When we got out the other end of the mud area and onto the dirt again the dirt was sticking to the wet mud all over my body, including the worst areas, my eyes and mouth. I tried to keep both my eyes and my mouth closed the best I could, but my eye lids and lips were still covered in mud and then dry dusty dirt as well.

Pete was not happy yet and turned the horse around and dragged me thru the mud again but this time he stopped just short of the dry dirt. I was just laying in the mud completely naked covered from head to toe on all sides of my body with a layer of mud, a layer of dry dirt, and another layer of mud.

Pete told me to get up and he pulled me slowly back towards the house which was over 125 yards from the mud area, so by the time we got there, with me baking in the hot sun, the mud was mostly dry on the outside, while on the inside I could still feel the wet slime of the mud.

I was mud colored brown from my toes to my hair and all thru my hair. I could open my eyes but kept blinking as the mud was all over my eye lashes and eye lids. I could taste the mud a bit even though I kept it out of my mouth, it was all over my lips and I had no way of getting it off.

When we got back to the front of the house, Pete took his end of the rope and thru it up over one of the rafters. It was one of the rafters that held up the front porch roof except that it stuck out past the roof line by about 6 feet over the yard.

Pete pulled the rope tight so that I had to stand on my tippy toes just to keep my feet on the ground and then Pete tied off the end of the rope so that I would just be hanging there in front of the house where everyone could see me, naked and all covered in mud.

Pete rode off on his horse and I just hung there baking in the hot sun. As time went by my legs were getting tired and my arms were getting sore from being pulled up like that over my head.

About 20 to 30 minutes later Rick came by and went over to the porch and came back with a cane. This was my first experience with a cane so I was not sure as what to expect. Rick started caning my ass and I struggled to move my ass away, but could not move much in this position.

The cane really stung, much different than the deep down type pain from the strap. But, it hurt almost as much in a different way. First I felt a tremendous sting and then a few seconds later I felt a burning sensation deep down in my muscle.

After about 20 hard stinging shots, Rick move to the other side and started a new from that side. The worst part of the caning was when the cane wrapped around the side of my ass and left a mean looking welt on the side of my ass where there was no fat to cushion the blow.

I noticed the same thing when I use to cane Sabrina and Ally and I always enjoyed the site of all those more angry looking welts much more then the welts left on the fatty part of their asses. Although, don't misunderstand, those welts on the nice plump parts of their ass's were real nice too.

As Rick continued to cane me I was OUCHING!!!!!!!!!!!!!! and yelling some and even screaming a little but I was able not to cry and I thought that was an achievement, for the "SISSY". The fact was that the cane had a real sting to it, but it was not killing me like that damn strap did.

Apparently that was not good enough for Rick as he

went over and got a thicker and longer cane. Rick came back around to where he could face me and he showed me the longer thicker cane.

Rick told me that this one should get me howling. Rick moved around behind me again and THWACK!!!!!!!!!!!!!!! Now that one really hurt. It stung a lot more and the deep down pain was twice as bad.

THWACK!!!!!!!!!!!!!   THWACK!!!!!!!!!!!!!!!!! THWACK!!!!!!!!!!!!!!! After I was hit with this longer and thicker cane I started to cry right away and was giving Rick just what her wanted.

The more I cried the harder it seemed that Rick would hit me, THWACK!!!!!!!!! THWACK!!!! THWACK!!!!!!!! THWACK!!!!!!!!!!!! Rick gave me about 20 more THWACKS!!!!!!!!!!!!!! on each side and I cried my heart out the whole time.

Rick stopped beating me and left me hanging there. I continued to cry for a few more minutes and if anything, this time, the tears washed the mud out of my eyes so my eyes felt better and I did not need to continue to blink.

Rick came back in about 30 minutes later and looked at me and said, "nigger huh?". Rick told me that I have forfeited my clothes for the next 10 days and that I had to stand in the corner during lunch for the next three days. Nigger, Huh? You SISSY!

I looked up at Rick, not wanting any more trouble, and said, yes Sir, I am sorry Sir. Rick unhooked me and I was allowed to go and shower and get back to work.

After I showered to get all the mud off me I walked back to the barn to meet John to work. At lunch time I put my wrist cuffs back on and stood in the corner with my wrists bound in front of me and higher then my head where my cuffs were attached to the hook in the wall.

As I stood there in the corner I could hear the guys talking to each other about what a sissy I am for crying like a little girl what Rick caned me. One guy even said that I should not be allowed to wear the man's shorts, I should be wearing panties.

So, I spent three more days standing in the corner for 30 minutes or so for lunch and I got to work and eat naked again for the next ten days. My ass continued to hurt for the next week or so and then the soreness left me. I still had tell tale bruises from all the welts for almost three weeks.

MY BIRTHDAY, MY PANTIES:

It was August 18th, my birthday. It was also Mindy's birthday and Cally's birthday and Ally birthday.

The last 10 days went by rather in a boring manner for me. I needed to spend those three days standing in the corner for lunch while many of the guys teased me about being a sissy.

Otherwise, I guess by then, they were use to me being naked with a punished ass on display as out of the 49 days that I had been at the Reform Farm so far, I was naked for thirty of those days, 10 days for each of my three punishments. I have also spend 10 days standing in the corner with my punishment marks on display.

As my 10 days of nakedness were up I was expecting my clothes back that morning. I was feeling sorry for myself as it was my 20th birthday and I was not allowed to see Cally that day as she was not permitted to visit again until September 1st.

I was looking forward to seeing Cally the following week on September 1st and was sure hoping that I could stay of trouble until then so I had clothes to wear and that I was not all marked up with punishments welts as that would disappoint Cally and I never wanted to disappoint Cally.

When I was getting ready to leave to go to the barn for

breakfast Rick showed up and I was expecting to get my pair of shorts and a T shirt to wear. However, as I looked towards Rick's hand I saw a small box instead.

Rick handled me the box and told me that it was a birthday present from Cally. I was so excited that Cally sent me something and that the Boss allowed me to receive it.

There was a card on the top of the box and as I opened the card to read it as Rick waited and watched for my reaction. However, as Rick did not have any clothes for me to wear, I almost opened my mouth and asked where my clothes were? But, I caught myself and shut up and tried to be patient.

I read Cally's birthday card, which said;

Dear Mort, happy birthday.

You know that I was not allowed to visit you this day or I would have been there with you to give you your present myself.

However, Mort, I understand that you have disappointed me with your Bad Boy behavior since I have seen you last and that is not acceptable to me, NOT EVEN A LITTLE BIT!

Therefore from now on, or until I allow you otherwise, you will wear the presents in the box that I have sent for you.

Mort, there will be no discussion in this matter, YOU ARE TO OBEY ME, PEROID!

Hopefully, Mort, when I see you on September first your behavior report will have improved, AS I FULLY EXPECT IT TO!!!!!!

To my surprise and shock, there were no shorts in the box. The box was full of women's panties of assorted colors. GREAT! Just GREAT!

I took the panties out of the box and looked at them and sort of smiled to Rick, as in "you got to be kidding! Rick looked at me and told to put a pair on. Then I actually opened my mouth and said, "these are girls panties! not shorts!

Really Rick said, If you do not want to war them it is alright with me. Then just come with me to the barn naked as you have been, yes Sir, I said, but I was real disappointed that I was not getting any shorts to wear.

However, I should have been more disappointed as to what was going to happen next because I did not obey Rick with a prompt yes Sir, followed by putting on the panties. Instead, as Rick and I walked to the barn I was thinking that I was to have breakfast and still be kept naked, but that was better than wearing panties.

However, just after Rick and I entered the barn, right in front of all the other guys, I was grabbed by Rick and Pete and bent over one of the picnic tables so that my ass was bend over the one end and then they attached the wrist cuffs to my wrists and attached the wrist cuffs to a rope at the other end of the picnic table and pulled the rope tight by tying it under the table.

So I was basically laying on the table with my legs at a

90 degree angle to the table so that my ass was out there as a perfect target to be abused or whatever they had in mind. After I was secured to the table Rick came over to me and showed me a wood paddle.

It was about what you would expect of a wood paddle. It was about two feet long including the handle and was about 8 inches wide and looked to be made from a hard wood which would make it much more solid and heavy and therefore hurt more than a lighter paddle. I guessed that was no surprise as it seemed around here that they wanted the punishments to hurt as much as they possible could.

Sadly, that reminded me that when it came to Sabrina and Ally, that I had the same theory, that I wanted their punishments to hurt as much as I could make them hurt. I always figured that half ass punishments were not that effective and besides, I enjoyed hurting them both. The more they struggled and screamed and cried the happier I was with their punishment.

Now, it seems that I am on the opposite side of that theory and that Rick and Pete and the Boss believe in the same theory, but now, that is not good for me. The only thing I can do to avoid more punishments is to obey, which so far I have not been real good at.

I always thought that Sabrina and Ally were pretty stupid to disobey me so often and get themselves punished so often, but I did not care as I loved to punish them. But, now, I see that it is just more of a natural thing within a person that tends to make you resist or at least ask questions.

The only way to get past that would be to gain enough self control of yourself to give up everything you think or want or care about and simply be totally obedient, to be totally submissive to others.

But, as I found out that was easier thought then done as my resistance mainly came from my internal and strong feeling about not being embarrassed or humiliated, then the desire to refuse the actual task itself.

Rick said to me, as he showed me the paddle, let me know when you are ready to wear the panties. I looked up at Rick and told him that I was ready now, but Rick just laughed and said that was good but that will not save my ass.

Rick said that I disobeyed him so I gave him a reason to have a real good time so he was going to have a real good time and that I can wear the panties some other day.

At that point the best I could hope for was not to cry in front of all the guys as that would be so, so humiliating for me. I don't know why I cry and they don't cry, but the fact was so far that I did cry. So I was going to try real hard this time not to cry.

Maybe the paddle would not hurt as much as that strap or that cane and I could get by with just yelling and groaning like the other guys do when they are punished?

Rick walked around behind me and SMACK!!!!!!!!! SMACK!!!!!!!!!!SMACK !!!!!!!!! SMACK!!!!!!!!! SMACK!!!!!!!!! SMACK!!!!!!!!!!! SMACK!!!!!! That is all that could be heard in the barn as the SMACK!!!!!!!! SMACK!!!!!!!! SMACK!!!!!!!!!!! was so loud.

SMACK!!!!!!!!!!!!   SMACK!!!!!!!!!!   SMACK!!!!!!!!! SMACK!!!!!!!!!! I could not even hear myself screaming OUCH! OUCH! OUCH! after each SMACK!!!!!!!!!! SMACK!!!!! Due to the echo in the barn and how fast the SMACKS!!! were coming, SMACK after SMACK after SMACK after hard SMACK!!!!!!!!!!!!

It did not take too many SMACKS!!!!!!!!!! with that paddle before I could not hold out any more and I burst into tears. So there I was crying like a girl in front of the all the other guys, no wonder they call me sissy. If I were them I would call me sissy also.

The guys started to clap and cheer for Rick for getting me to cry while they chanted SISSY! SISSY! SISSY! SISSY! SISSY! SISSY! I could feel the humiliation growing in me as I knew when this paddling was over that I would need to get up and they would see my tears dripping down my face and that would make the crying all that more humiliating for me.

I did think that, SMACK!!!!!!!!!!! SMACK!!!!!!!! SMACK!!!!!!!!!! SMACK!!!!!!!!! SMACK!!!!!!!! SMACK!!!!!!!!, crying made the punishment a little easier to take, however. SMACK!!!! SMACK!!! SMACK!!! SMACK!!!! SMACK!!!

To make a long paddling story short, Rick beat me with that paddle for about 10 minutes or about 150 swats, at about 15 swats per minute, or one swat every 4 seconds. I could do nothing except lay there and take that beating, yet another beating, my fourth beating and I have been there for less than two months. I guess like I expected from Sabrina and Ally, I had better learn to obey and learn real quick.

As soon as Rick finished beating me with that paddle, he untied my hands and helped me to stand up. I would have preferred to lay there until I stopped crying, but I guess Rick wanted me to be stood up so that everyone could see me stand there crying my eyes out to prove to all the guys that I am the sissy, that they now call me.

That is just what Rick did too, he made me stand there in front of all the guys while they apparently enjoyed watching me cry like a big sissy. All the guys started clapping and hollering again and calling me a sissy all over again. In spite of the pain in my ass and the humiliation of being punished in front of all those guys, I still felt a greater humiliation from crying.

After I calmed down, which took about two minutes or so, Rick took me over to one of the corners so that I could stand in the corner while all the guys could see my well paddled ass. Rick hooked my hands in the usual manner above my head so that I was stretched out but that I had none of my weight being held up by arms.

I stood there in that corner still having trouble breathing as my nose was still clogged from all of my crying. It took about an half hour for all the guys to finish their breakfast and to get their job assignments for the day and for the barn to empty out. Only then was I released and was allowed to have breakfast and to go to work.

As Rick released me he told me that I needed to stand in the corner for the next five mornings for breakfast, yes sir, as I bowed my head to look at the ground in shame and disappointment. Then Rick told me that I needed to come to him in ten days and ask him real nice for permission to wear my new panties. Yes Sir.

At lunch time, now that all the guys actually saw me cry themselves all the comments about me being a sissy were back to the point where they actually starting calling me sissy and not by my real name.

Ten days later when I showed up to the barn for breakfast you could still see the bruises from that paddling but they were mostly faded to a lighter color of black and blue, but my ass was not really sore anymore.

However, for the last 10 days, everyone, including my work buddy, John, called me sissy, like it was my real name.

So, I have been there on the Reform Farm now for just under 60 days. During those 60 days I have been punished 4 times. Which meant that I was naked for 40 of the 60 days. I was naked so much I was beginning to enjoy being naked. I actually like being naked. However, I did not like being naked when everyone else had clothes on as I found that continually embarrassing.

I started to get nervous and did not sleep well that 10th night as I knew that I needed to go and see Rick the next morning and ask him for permission to wear the panties. I actually would have preferred to stay naked as I thought the panties would be much more embarrassing then being naked.

The next morning I walked to the barn for breakfast and

to see Rick and ask for my panties. I embarrassing as I knew it would be I had no choice and I did go up to Rick as I arrived at the barn and asked Rick, very politely, if I could please have those panties to wear. Rick looked at me and laughed, but said sure and he pulled a pair of black panties out of his pocket and gave them to me.

I put the panties on and found them to feel really good against my skin. Then I remembered that I also enjoyed that feeling on the cruse with Cally when she made me wear panties for her.

However, that was the good part of having to wear the panties. As you may have guessed, if you are a sissy? I started to get an erection which could be clearly seen thru the panties.

Rick noticed right away and grabbed me by my arm and took me over to the center of the hallway and very loudly announced to all the other guys who were there for breakfast, "LOOK GUYS, OUR SISSY REALLY LIKES HER NEW PANTIES!"

All the guys started looking at me and by then I had a full erection which showed the guys two things, one that my inner self liked wearing the panties and two that I had a very small cock compared to them.

The guys started clapping and whistling at me and calling out sissy, sissy, sissy, sissy, again and again. To make things worse, even though that increased my humiliation greatly, my erection did not go down.

Rick allowed me to eat my breakfast and go to work in my new panties. At lunch time the guys did not say much about my panties, but I could hear a few of them talking about me by using the sissy name.

After that, all the guys called me sissy like it was my real name, all the time. After a while, I thought that the guys all forgot my real name as even Rick and Pete called me sissy all the time.

At the end of the day when I got back to my room I found the box of panties that Cally sent me for my birthday which had 10 more pairs of panties in several different colors. I assumed that meant that from now on that I would being wearing panties every day and that Cally did not intend to let me wear the men's short at all, at least any time soon.

I thought that the worst part about the panties was that when I would sweat when I was working. My fears were confirmed later that day as I noticed that the panties would stick to my skin to the point where the guys would be able to see thru them to a degree and that the panties would form to the shape of my cock providing no real privacy at all.

The white panties and the pink panties were the worst as you could almost see thru them even before I got them all sweaty. But, what could I do, everyone called me sissy anyway and now I guess I look the part. At least I was protected from being attached or being used by any of the guys. So, getting past the constant embarrassment, I did not feel unsafe.

On August 29td, while I was cleaning the barn with john and I was thinking that things were very quiet around the farm these days. Everyone seemed to know why they were there on the farm and found it better then to be in a real prison. However, none of the guys that were on the farm were guilty of any violent crimes. Mostly drug crimes, or sex crimes, or theft crimes.

However, after breakfast just after John and I finished sweeping the floors Rick came into the barn with two of the guys following him. The two guys apparently got into a quick fight and one guy said something to the other guy and that guy punched him and they ended up on the ground fighting.

So Rick brought them both to the barn to punish them. I had never seen any of the other guys get punished before so I was curious and wanted to watch. I asked the cook if it was alright and he told it that it was fine and in fact they encouraged others to watch punishments as they thought it would scare the other guys into behaving better.

Rick told the guy who opened his mouth that he was going to punish him first. He had both men pull out a bench that was over in the corner. It was a punishment bench just like the one I had at home that I use to bind Sabrina and Ally to when I had such a good time strapping or caning their asses until they had welts on top of welts and they were screaming and crying as hard as they could. OH!!!!!!!! The good ole days!

Anyway, Rick had the guy take off his shorts and I had to admit that his cock was a lot bigger them mine. Rick bound the big mouth guy to the bench with the same system I used with Sabrina and Ally and Cally with the four wrist cuffs and ankle cuffs hooked to each leg of the bench and a wide leather strap across their his waist. The guy had a real nice muscular ass to go with that nice big cock of his.

Then Rick got out the big thick strap and the CRACK!!!!!!!! was so loud inside the barn I thought I was going to need ear plugs. CRACK!!!!!!!!!!!!!!!!!!!!! CRACK!!!!!!!!!!!!!!!!!!!!!!! CRACK !!!! Rick beat that guys ass but good with CRACK!!!!!!!!!! after CRACK!!!!! after CRACK!!!!!!!!!! after CRACK!!!!!!!!!!!!!!!!!!!!. Every one of those licks left a long big red welt all the way around to the side of his ass just like I use to do with Sabrina and Ally.

Before I knew what was happening I noticed that I had an erection. That was just great as those tan panties I was wearing that day were showing the obvious, that I got a hard on from watching Rick give that guy with the nice ass a good sound strapping and I was enjoying watching it.

I also noticed as Rick was changing sides to strap the guy from the other side that after about 20 or 25 licks the guy made a lot of noise, by saying OUCH!!!!!!!! or AHHH!!!!!!!!!! or he would moan, and he would grit his teeth, but he did not cry.

Rick gave him another 20 or 25 licks from the other side

and let him up. Rick finished strapping the first guy, the one with the big mouth after about 50 or maybe 60 hard licks altogether. As Rick let him up he was a little off balance so he held on to a support post.

Meanwhile, Rick had the next guy, the punching guy, take off his shorts and he too had a much bigger cock them me. He also had a great ass, even nicer then the first guy. I was still trying to stay to the side so no one would notice that I had an erection and that was working out pretty good for now.

Then Rick surprised me by telling the first guy, the guy with the already strapped ass, that he could strap the second guy as hard as he wishes as the guy punched him. The first guy was only about 5' 9" or 5' 10" and was about 190 pounds and had plenty of muscles, but was much smaller the Rick, the giant, I called Rick and Pete.

So, I figured that the first guy could not hit the second guy as hard as Rick, but I was sure he was going to try to punish that guy who punched him and broke his lip which was still bleeding a little bit. Apparently Rick was going to let the guy strap the puncher as long as he wanted to as Rick did not give him any amount of licks.

The first guy went right to work and hit the second guy with that long thick strap as hard as he could and just kept at it for a good 10 minutes until Rick finally told him to stop. I loved watching the whole thing and maintained my erection though out. I was so happy that no one was paying any attention to me or they would have clearly seen it thru my thin panties.

However, once again, the second guy did not cry, rather he yelled some and OUCHED!!!!!!!!!! some and moaned some and grunted some, but no crying and no tears.

It was not what I was use to with Sabrina or Ally where there was plenty of screaming and so many tears. Then, it was not the same as me either, plenty of screaming and yelling and then many, so many tears. I guess I am a sissy.

As soon as the second strapping was over I ran into the bathroom so no one would see my erection. I used a towel and ran cold water on it and use the cold water to make my erection go away. At least by the time the other guys came for lunch my penis was back to it obvious small size.

When I came back from the bathroom both guys were standing in two different corners that were not that far apart. The guys could look over and see the other one if that wanted too. I was just looking at their nice bodies and those two great looking asses and I started to get hard again. So, I stopped looking and tried to pay attention to what I needed to do to keep my penis down.

The first guy, the big mouth guy, had to stand in the corner for three lunches including that first day. The second guy, the punching guy, had to stand in the corner for five days for lunch. Both guys had to be naked for the next 10 days.

I was thinking about that punishment later as I was cleaning up after lunch and I was wondering why Rick strapped the first guy and not the second. Then I remembered about the old saying, "you scratch my back and I will scratch yours".

That saying comes from old time English war ships when someone was to be whipped, the guy with the whip would just try to whip the other guy with just the tips of the whip that would still cause him to bleed but not hurt that much, In other words, SCRATCH, him.

Then when the other guy would get in trouble for something he would expect the same type of cheating on the whipping. They figured that if the guy screamed a lot the officers would think he was getting a real whipping and not think that they were being fooled.

So, in other words, in this case, Rick was most likely afraid that if he let them punish each other that they would cheat and try not to hurt on another all that much. So, Rick strapped the first guy so that he would have no reason not to punish the second guy as hard as he could. I guess Rick was pretty smart when it came to this punishment stuff.

It was September 1st and I had been embarrassed just thinking about that day for the last three days, as what I assumed turned out to be true, that I would have to meet Cally wearing only my panties. I chose the black panties that day as if nothing else, black covers better as black does not reflect light. Pete told me that Cally would be here at 2 pm.

I walked slowly from the barn to the house that day as I was full of mixed emotions. I was full of shame for Cally seeing me here at a prison labor camp to begin with.

But, that afternoon Cally was also going to find out that I was punished yet again and that time it was because I did not obey her and put on the panties. I knew that would not make Cally happy, which in turn would not make me happy. Nevertheless, at the same time, I was just thrilled to see Cally. Cally was my only highlight in my life at that point in time.

As I approached the house I could see Cally sitting on the porch waiting for me. I walked up the stairs of the porch but I was having trouble looking at Cally, as I felt so embarrassed. Cally got up and came over to me and gave me a kiss and told me that she was very happy to see me again. I just smiled waiting to see what else she was going to say.

Cally looked down at my panties. Cally told me to turn

around and as I did Cally checked out how my ass looked in the panties. I turned back around and Cally looked at me and smiled and said nice panties Mort, I like them, I think you shall always wear panties from now on.

I did not know if I was going to cry or laugh as why would I ever wear panties from now on? I won't be here that long, only four years, I thought. Nevertheless, Cally did make me feel less conspicuous about the panties in front of her, so that was a good thing.

I told Cally I looked forward to see her more than I could explain, but not like this I added. No Mort! The panties are nice and I actually like them on you. And I am serious, I will always have you wear panties for me, from now on. I could not explain what the hell Cally was talking about, but oddly enough, I got an erection.

Cally noticed my penis growing in my panties right away, even before I was all the way hard. Cally even stepped back and watched my cock grow thru my panties as she smiled the whole time. When I was fully hard, Cally stepped forward again and used her hand to feel my cock. Cally looked in my eyes and just smiled again.

Cally asked me if I had been punished for anything since she saw me last. I lowered my head and looked at the ground in shame and told Cally twice. WHAT FOR, MORT?

I told Cally about my nigger comment and the caning and then I told Cally about the panties and the paddling. TURN AROUND, MORT!

As I turned around Cally lowered my panties so she

could see what was left of the bruises from the paddle. Cally took a nice long look and then put her hand on my ass and felt my ass cheeks as well. I was not sure what that was about, but Cally just pulled my panties back up and told me to turn around.

As I turned around and faced Cally, Cally pointed her finger in my face and scolded me, DID I NOT TELL YOU TO BEHAVE, MORT? Yes Cally. SO, MORT, DID YOU OBEY ME? No, Cally. WELL THEN, MORT, THERE WILL BE NO BLOW JOBS FOR YOU TODAY, NO KISSES, NO NOTHING, NOT UNTIL YOU LEARN TO BE OBEDIENT TO ME!!!!!!!!!

Alright, Mort lets go inside to the office. I followed Cally into the office like a shamed little boy, as I felt so humiliated to have Cally scold me like that. However, Cally was correct, I did not obey her and I knew that her scolding of me was well deserved. But, that understanding did not lessen the humiliation I felt.

As we walked into the office, Cally did not sit on the couch, rather she went behind the desk and sat down. Cally told me to stand in front of the desk. So, now, Cally was treating me like my Boss and not my best friend in this world.

Cally asked me if I cried like a little girl during both the caning and the paddling. If Cally was trying to humiliate me even more, she was sure doing a good job. Yes Cally, I cried every time that I was punished and that is why everyone calls me sissy.

Cally asked me if it was hard to take a caning like that and I told her it sure was. So, Cally asked? How do you think that Ally and Sabrina felt while you were beating them with a cane? I told Cally that I got her point.

Cally? Yes Mort, I am real sorry that I punished you like that, I am sorry I ever hurt you. As Cally always does, she surprised me again. Don't be Mort, you and the way you both punished and rewarded me was the best thing that has ever happened to me in my life. I intend to have a great life now that you have taught me how to behave properly.

Mort, I deserved every one of those punishments and you always punished me with love, not like you beat Sabrina and Ally, so don't ever apologize for helping guide me thru a difficult and confusing time in my life. As Cally was finishing her speech to me, she started to tear up. WOW! was all I could think. I sure did not expect to hear that from Cally.

After a minute or so break for Cally to wipe her eyes, Cally, continued. Mort, you also punished Sabrina and Ally many times and they deserved it also. In fact, Mort, Ally is now going to go to college because of you and the way you punished her and for the reasons you punished her.

Sabrina, she was a terrible maid until you started to punish her. Now, she is much happier and better maid and provides better for her family.

I can tell you Mort that there are parts of both Sabrina and Ally that appreciate some of your efforts. However, with them, you just went too far. Mort, can you stand there and tell me that you fucked Sabrina and Ally in the ass and hurt them as much as you could for any other reason other than you enjoyed it? No, Cally, I can't.

Mort, are you going to tell me that you made Sabrina and Ally become experts at sucking your cock for you for any other reason then you enjoyed it? No, Cally, I cannot.

Well, Mort, I am glad you recognize this as we are making good progress. So, Mort, now you just need to accept that you are here being punished for those crimes against Sabrina and Ally. Not for the good things you tried to do by punishing them. I nodded in agreement with Cally. I knew she was right, Cally was always right.

Alright Mort, now we just need to get you to the point where you can be obedient and everyone can more on to a happier life. MORT, YOU DO WANT TO LEARN TO OBEY ME DON'T YOU? Yes Cally.

I really just agreed with Cally as she was taking that stern tone with me and I felt so bad to begin with so I was not about to disagree with anything she said. However, my cock started to grow in my panties again and Cally had a clear view as she watched it get hard for the second time in about 10 minutes.

So, I guess I am not kidding anyone but myself. I was never happier then when I obey every single thing Cally ever told me to do during our last year together. So, I guess that I do wish I would learn to obey Cally. We both would probably be happier that way.

Additionally, When Cally is stern with me like she has

been today, It really does excite me and I enjoy seeing Cally like that.

Cally and I chatted about all sorts of other things as I stood there in front of her wearing my black silk panties while I was embarrassed as I could be for disobeying Cally and getting scolded by Cally and having my cock tell her that I enjoy her dominate tone with me.

Well, Cally said, I am going to cut this visit short as you behavior has not been what I had expected, Mort. Perhaps, next time I come here, you have better give me a better report.

OH! WAIT! I almost forgot Mort. That issue you asked me to look into about LeMond. Yes Cally? Well Mort, it turns out that the Boss was correct and LeMond was covering for someone else. LeMond will most likely be released in a few days as the police now have the correct person.

I am glad Cally, that is good news. Yes Mort, and in spite of you poor behavior and my disappoint in you, you did a nice thing here for this LeMond, a real nice thing. Thank you, Cally.

Cally? Yes Mort? That reminds me. I saw Rick the other day sitting in a corner sort of crying as he seemed real upset. Since then, he has had something heavy on his mind. Please have that detective look into Rick's life and find out what happened in his family as he himself looks alright to me. Alright, Mort, I will do that and let you know.

I was walking Cally to her car when the Boss drove up

and got out of his car and said hello to Cally and asked how are things going? Right there in front of me, Cally told the Boss that she likes me in panties so I should always wear panties from now on.

Then Cally told the Boss that she was not happy with my behavior and that she scolded me and that he will see better behavior from me.

I was about as humiliated as I could be. The Boss looked at me and smiled in a laughing manner and then told Cally it was nice to see her again and to have a nice day.

When we walked over to Cally's car, Cally looked at me again with tears in her eyes and reminded me that she expects me to be brave to be obedient and accept my punishment as it is deserved, as after all Mort, you do deserve to be punished. I know Cally, I know.

Which an erection again in my panties again, Cally felt it once more with her hand and gave me a nice smile and then a nice kiss on the lips and said goodbye. I will see you again in about two weeks. I just smiled and started to get all teary eyed again and tried to tell myself again that I was a man and men don't cry, but I guess we all know that that ship has sailed.

ME, THE BOSS, AND THE STRAP:

September 2nd, Just after lunch Pete told me that the Boss wanted to see me and that he did not sound happy. I walked down to the house and the closer I got the more nervous I got.

I could only assume that the Boss found about me having everyone checked out or he found out about me having LeMond checked out and he was not happy.

The Boss was sitting on the porch and as I walked up the steps and you wished to see me Boss? The Boss looked at me and told me that he was only going to ask me this once! Did you or did you not hired someone to check me out, Mort?

Yes Sir. Did you or did you not understand the rule about not doing anything unless you were told to do it, Mort? Yes Sir. Well, Mort, I am very unhappy with you and my strap is going to explain just how unhappy I am.

The Boss got up and picked up his strap off the floor where he had it resting for me to see and took me over to the hitching post and then told me to take off my panties and lay over, yes Sir. I was plenty scared and my legs were starting to shake already and I was afraid that I was going to cry even before the Boss punished me with that big thick strap.

The Boss secured my feet with ankle cuffs to the ground pins behind me and then secured my hands with wrist cuffs to the pins in the ground in front of me. A familiar position that I was very unhappy to be in again.

Without another word from the Boss, CRACK!!!!!! CRACK!!!!!!!!! CRACK!!!!!!!!! CRACK!!!!!!! CRACK!!!!!!! CRACK!!!!!! CRACK!!!!! CRACK!!!!!! I was not sure that this strapping did not hurt any more then the last time, but it sure hurt just as much.

For the next 10 minutes all that was heard was CRACK!!!! CRACK!!!!! CRACK!!!!! CRACK!!!!! CRACK!!!!! CRACK!!!!!! CRACK!!!!!! CRACK!!!!!!! I thought that the Boss was correct that they do like to punish the inmates. CRACK!!!!!!!! CRACK!!!!!!!!!! CRACK!!!!!!!!!!! CRACK!!!!!

The Boss was strapping me about a hard as he could and if he thought that he was punishing me and teaching me a lesson and hurting me as much as he could? The Boss was sure correct as this was just simply horrible, it hurt so much and I could not do anything about it.

CRACK!!!!! CRACK!!!!!!! CRACK!!!!!! CRACK!!!!! CRACK!!!!! CRACK!!!! CRACK!!!!!! CRACK!!!!!!! CRACK!!!!!!! CRACK!!!!!!!!!! All I could do was lay there over that wood rail and suffer and cry and cry and cry and cry some more.

I guess this is what the Boss meant when he said that they all enjoy their job of punishing Bad Boys as I was being punished and punished and punished some more, like I never thought possible.

CRACK!!!! CRACK!!!!!! CRACK!!!!! CRACK!!!!!

CRACK!!!!!! CRACK!!!!!! CRACK!!!!! CRACK!!!!! CRACK!!!!!!!!!! CRACK!!!!!!!!!!! CRACK!!!!!! CRACK!!!!!! CRACK!!!!! The Boss was taking his time and making sure each and every CRACK!!!!! was hurting me to the maximum.

I thought that after about a full 10 minutes and about 50 welts that covered my entire ass and both sides of my ass from nothing but CRACK!!! CRACK!!!!!! CRACK!!!!!! CRACK!!!!!!!!!! CRACK!!!!! CRACK!!!!! CRACK!!!!

The long strapping was getting my ass so swollen that it was not hurting so much anymore. Only where the tail of the strap would wrap around and hit the side of my ass was still hurting and still hurting a whole lot.

The Boss, being well experienced at beating his inmates understood that he could no longer hurt me very much by continuing to strap my ass. So the Boss moved down to my legs.

The Boss started strapping the back of my thighs with the same viscous CRACK!! CRACK!!!! CRACK!!!! CRACK!!!! CRACK!!! CRACK!!!! CRACK!!!! CRACK!!! CRACK!!!! CRACK!!!!! CRACK!!!! CRACK!!!! CRACK!!!! CRACK!!!

The CRACKING!!!! just continued as I screamed in terrible pain and cried and cried and cried some more. As the back of my thighs had no fat to pad them, not only did the welts seem to hurt even more, I could feel some small pieces of my skin being torn off with some of the LICKS!!!

The Boss just continued to beat me with that big black strap and gave me about 5 more minutes or 25 more licks from the right side and the Boss moved over to my left side and CRACK!!!! CRACK!!!! CRACK!!! CRACK!!!! CRACK!!!! CRACK!!!! CRACK!!!! CRACK!!! CRACK!!! CRACK!!!

The Boss continued to beat me and beat me and beat me with that big fat strap. I was just covered with big red welts from my ass to my knees. I was going to be nothing but black and blue for weeks afterwards.

After another 5 minutes passed and another 25 welts were added to my body. I was screaming so loud and for so long that I was starting to lose my voice. I really did not think that the Boss was happy with me for having him checked out.

The Boss stopped strapping me and after about 100 licks I was sure he was done as that was some beating. That was for sure the worst beating I have ever had and by far the worst beating I have ever seen, even in a place like this where punishments like this are common.

The Boss walked around to the front of me and knelt down on one knee and grabbed the back of my head by the hair and pulled my head up so that I could see him or he could seeing me crying.

The Boss looked at me and told me that I was just a rich little piece of shit that needs to learn to mind his own business. NOW, that I have your attention, MORTON, I am going to show you what real punishment is!

At that the Boss went around behind me again and CRACK!!!! CRACK!!!! CRACK!!!! CRACK!!!! CRACK!!!! CRACK!!!! CRACK!!!! CRACK!!!! CRACK!!!! The Boss had nowhere else to strap me except on my back and he was using that heavy thick strap to do just that as the Boss just strapped me without any mercy that day.

CRACK!!!! CRACK!!!!!! CRACK!!!! CRACK!!!!!!! CRACK!!!!!! CRACK!!!!! CRACK!!!!! CRACK!!!!! CRACK!!!!! CRACK!!!!! CRACK!!!!! CRACK!!!!! CRACK!!! CRACK!!!! CRACK!!!! CRACK!!!! CRACK!!!! CRACK!!!! CRACK!!!!

The Boss just beat me and beat me and beat me some more that day. He gave me another 25 CRACKS!!!!!! CRACK!!!! CRACK!!!! CRACK!!!! CRACK!!! from the left side and then went around to the right side and CRACK!!!! CRACK!!!!! CRACK!!!! CRACK!!! CRACK!!!!! CRACK!!!! CRACK!!!!

The Boss finished me off with 25 more welts from the left side and I don't think, except for my kidney area on my lower back area, that there was any white skin left between my shoulders and my knees as there was nothing but welts.

The strapping lasted about 30 minutes altogether and I lost my voice shortly after the Boss starting with that strap on my back, but I cried almost the entire time, basically in an hysterical manner.

The Boss finally stopped strapping me and just walked away and left me to cry my eyes out and suffer in unbelievable pain. Pain that I never knew existed. Terrible pain, just terrible. I must have been given about 150 licks as the Boss was letting me know loud and very clear that he did not appreciate me having him checked out.

The Boss came back around in front of me again and lifted up my head again with the back of my hair and as the Boss threw the strap on the ground next to me and said Mort, it was a good thing at least you were honest with me, or I may have been angry instead of just teaching you to be more obedient.

The Boss left me there to cry and I continued to cry for maybe five minutes before I was able to stop. The Boss came back in about 15 minutes and unhooked me and helped me to my feet.

The Boss told me that I needed to go to the barn and stand in the corner for 30 minutes for lunch and 30 minutes for dinner for the next 10 days and as I knew, no clothes for ten days. Additionally, Mort, you are to stand in the corner with your hands bound behind your back.

As I walked around over the next 10 days, naked, showing off my well strapped ass, my well strapped back, and my well strapped legs, I still could not decide if I would prefer to stay naked, or go back to wearing the panties. However, it did not really matter what I thought as it was not my decision. Apparently it was Cally's and Cally was going to chose the panties.

As I stood in the corner with my hands bound behind my back I realized that it was harder to stand in the corner that way. With my hands bound in front of me and hooked to the wall, I could lean on the wall somewhat, which took some weight of my legs.

However, with my hands bound behind my back, I had all my weight on my feet and I had to balance myself as well. So, standing in the corner this way was much harder and much more uncomfortable.

I could hear some of the guys behind me talking about how badly I was punished and they wondered what I could have done wrong to get the Boss that angry with me as they had never seen anyone punished that severely before.

JOB CHANGE:

The next morning, on September 3nd, after breakfast I was told that I would not be working with John any longer that now I was to help the cook serve the meals and clean up the barn after all the meals. After all Pete told me, if you are going to be a sissy, you may as well learn to act like one.

So, now I was the food servant. Now I had to get up earlier and be in the barn by 7:30 am to set all the tables. Then when the guys arrived, while they ate, I had to serve them by filling their drinks, or getting them seconds, or getting them another napkin, etc. The best part of all of this was that I got to do it while I wore my panties and everyone called me by calling out, SISSY!

After all the guys left for their work detail in the morning the cook and I got to eat. Then I had to clean all the tables and put all the plates and cups and silverware in the dishwasher and get them ready for lunch. I helped the cook clean whatever he told me to clean and then it was time to set the table for lunch and start all over again.

Between lunch and dinner I had a little more free time after cleaning up after lunch before I needed to set the table for dinner and start the process all over again. By the time I cleaned up after dinner it was about 7:30 at night and I would go back to my room.

So this was my new schedule, but what else did I have to do, I had no TV, no computer, no phone, not that I wanted to talk to anyone anyway. However, 20 days later when I got back to my room I found that the TV had a power cord and there was a note on the TV which said that I could now have the TV power cord as I have been obedient for 20 straight days.

Well, that was good news I thought, but by the time I got back to my room in the evening I only had time to watch one or two shows and I would fall asleep as I had to get up early every morning. But, hay, I had a TV now and I have not been beaten for three weeks, so things were looking up as far as the obedience thing was going.

I was getting use to serving all the guys and in spite of them all calling me sissy they treated me pretty good and were very respectful towards my position as the lowly clean up and service kid.

This is the end of my story for now, Please watch out for The Bad Boy Gets Punished, Two. A sissy maid missy bad boy series part five, for my continuing story.

THE BAD BOY GETS PUNISHED, TWO

A SISSY MAID MISSY BAD BOY SERIES, PART FIVE

We get an update about LeMond, and I get another chat with the Boss.

Cally visits and I get a big surprise, not in a good way.

October 1st, I was severely punished in front of the "FAMILY"

I finally got new clothes, and not just panties, but was I better off?

Another chat with the Boss, this time about Rick, was I in trouble again?

Thanksgiving on the Reform Farm, surprise and discovery.

THE WORST AND BEST DAY OF MY LIFE, How could I be so stupid?

Cally and the whip, poor me.

More Cally surprises, they never seem to stop coming.

My six month punishment in front of the girls.

And, much more in, THE BAD BOY GETS PUNISHED, PART TWO.

A sissy maid missy bad boy series, part five

SPANKING DIARY

A sissy maid missy series, part one

SPANKINGS AND SUBMISSION, TO MY WIFE

A sissy amid missy series, part two

A SISSY MAIDS LIFE

A sissy maid missy series, part three

A SISSY MAIDS LIFE, TWO

A sissy maid missy series, part four

A SISSY MAIDS LIFE, THREE

A sissy maid missy series, part five

The Bad Boy and His French Maids

A sissy maid missy bad boy series, part one

The Bad Boy and His French Maids, Two

A sissy maid missy bad boy series, part two

The Bad Boy and His French Maids, Three

A sissy maid missy bad boy series, part three

The Bad Boy Gets Punished

A sissy maid missy bad boy series, part four

The Bad Boy Gets Punished, Two

A sissy maid missy bad boy series, part five

The Bad Boy, The sissy Maid

A sissy maid missy bad boy series, part six

The Bad Boy, The sissy Maid, Tw

A sissy maid missy bad boy series, part seven

The Bad Boy, The sissy Maid, Three

A sissy maid missy bad boy series, part Eight

The Bad Boy, The Sissy Maid, Four

A sissy maid missy bad boy series, part Nine

The Bad Boy, The Sissy Maid, Five

A sissy maid missy bad boy series, part Ten

The Bad Boy, the Sissy Maid, Six

A sissy maid missy bad boy series, part eleven

Ally's Gone

A sissy maid missy bad boy series, part twelve